ULT...

MOTIVE

D0804410

DEC - - 2009

HU

ULTERIOR MOTIVE

roy glenn

URBAN BOOKS

http://www.urbanbooks.net

This is a work of fiction. Any references or similarities to actual events, real people, living or dead, or to real locales are intended to give the novel a sense of reality. Any similarity in other names, characters, places, and incidents is entirely coincidental.

URBAN SOUL is published by

Urban Books
1199 Straight Path
West Babylon, NY 11704

ISBN-13: 978-1-59983-080-3
ISBN-10: 1-59983-080-9

First Printing: October 2008

10 9 8 7 6 5 4 3 2 1

Printed in the United States of America

ULTERIOR MOTIVE

Chapter 1

It was late on Thursday afternoon when Marcus Douglas finally left the office. He had spent most of the day preparing for the trial of a client, Nadia Whitfield, who was charged with murder and armed robbery. She was involved with three others in a bank robbery. During the course of the robbery, a teller had hit the silent alarm. When the police arrived at the bank, Nadia promptly surrendered to the first cop that came at her. The getaway driver, who saw the police arrive and take Nadia into custody, quickly left the scene. When the police entered the bank, the three members of the gang opened fire on them. One of the robbers, Calvin Slinger, killed a bank guard, while another robber's wild shots killed the other member of the gang. The police killed the second robber and the teller that was behind him.

After reviewing the case, Marcus had attempted to have her tried separately from the rest of the gang. So far, his attempts had been unsuccessful.

He was on his way to see Angela Pettybone, an old friend from college at CCNY in New York. In those days, Angela was his best friend Darnel's girlfriend, but Marcus was secretly in love with Angela. The three of them used to hang out together. It was rare that you saw one without the other two. They were so close that at times Marcus felt like Angela was his girlfriend too.

After graduation, the three went their separate ways. Marcus and Darnel kept in touch with each other while Marcus attended Columbia Law School, but lost touch when Darnel moved to California. He never saw or heard from Angela and had pretty much forgotten about her until his personal assistant, Janise, told him that Angela Pettybone was holding for him.

"What—what did you say?" Marcus asked her to repeat what he knew he heard.

"I said, there is an Angela Pettybone holding for you on line two. She says she's an old friend of yours from college."

"Thank you, Janise," Marcus said, and a rush of memories of the feelings he'd had for her washed over him. He took a deep breath and picked up the phone.

"Angela, how are you?"

"I'm in trouble and I need your help, Marcus."

"What's wrong, Angela?"

"I really don't want to talk over the phone. I need to talk to you in person."

"Where are you living these days?"

"I'm here in Atlanta."

"Really?"

"I moved here about six years ago."

"Six years, huh?"

"Closer to seven. But, Marcus, I really have to talk to you."

"No problem," Marcus said, and looked at his watch. "You could come into the office anytime tomorrow. Just call and let Janise know—" Marcus started, but Angela interrupted him.

"Marcus, please, I need to talk to you as soon as you can. Could you come to my house?"

So there he was, driving out I-20 to Angela's house in a suburb of Atlanta. Along the way Marcus made a promise to himself that no matter how he felt about Angela these days, he would not get involved with her on any other level but business. His track record with women in general, and with women clients in particular, had not been too great.

Marcus had gotten involved with a former client named Yvonne Haggler. She had been working as a courier and was trying to get out of the business. She and Marcus shared an adventure together that he would remember for the rest of his life. An adventure that left him knowing that there was only one way out of that type of life.

Then there was former supermodel Carmen Taylor. She wasn't a client but the sister of a woman who was the wife of his client, Roland Ferguson. He was on trial for the murder of his wife, Desireé Taylor Ferguson, Carmen's sister, and her lover. Roland was accused of beating them both to death with a golf club in a cabin in north Georgia. His time spent with Carmen led to a love that Marcus thought would last forever. It ended when Carmen got restless and caught the bug to restart her modeling career and moved to Europe. They grew apart because of the distance between them, and Panthea Daniels.

Panthea Daniels was a client who came to see him about divorcing her husband, who she believed was having an affair. From the moment she stepped into his office, they were drawn to each other like bees to the sweet nectar of flowers.

After seeing pictures of the woman, Panthea, who was quite shaken by the experience, left Marcus's office and said, "It's not every day you see your husband's mistress." The next day Panthea was arrested and was accused of murdering her husband's mistress. Their time together was filled with passion, as the two explored their sexuality to the fullest.

Marcus brought the relationship to an abrupt end when he found out that Panthea was not the person she presented herself to be. That decision didn't sit well with Panthea. She was desperately in love with Marcus and planned to spend the rest of her life with him. Since her trial ended five months ago, Panthea had made her displeasure with the situation felt. It was limited to pleading phone calls, unannounced visits to his office and home, and the occasional interruption of a business meeting. However, it had been more than two months since Marcus had heard anything from Panthea Daniels. He assumed she had finally moved on with her life, a fact that suited him just fine. All that strengthened Marcus's resolve not to become involved with Angela Pettybone on any level other than business. *No matter how fine she looks.*

When Marcus got to the address that Angela gave him, he parked the car and walked toward the house. As he walked, he looked at the house and was glad that Angela seemed to be doing well for herself. He rang the bell and waited nervously. When the door opened, Angela stood in the doorway.

For Marcus, it was as if time had stood still, and out of nowhere the rush of feelings that he hadn't felt in years all came into focus. Now Angela Pettybone stood before him, looking every bit as beautiful as the last time he saw her. Her caramel skin looked as if a day hadn't passed since the last time he saw her. Her silky black hair was still parted down the middle and hung off her shoulders. Angela's eyes seemed to dance just as they did each time he looked into his. And her smile; there were days he thought he'd die without seeing that smile.

"Marcus!" she shrieked, and immediately threw her arms around Marcus and kissed him on the cheek. Angela took a step back and looked at him. As soon as she had hung up the phone with Marcus, Angela knew that she was probably overreacting, but there he was. And it was good to see him. If nothing else, it would give her a chance to catch up with an old friend. "It is so good to see you. Come in, come in."

Once they were inside, Angela looked at Marcus again. "You look good, Marcus. Like you haven't changed a bit since college."

"Well, I have put on a few pounds since then, but look at you. Angela, you are absolutely beautiful." He paused. "You put on a few pounds since then too." Angela took a playful swing at her old friend. Marcus always did know how to push her buttons. "But they are all well placed. You look fantastic," he said with his eyes glued to Angela's cleavage, and hugged her again.

"I'm glad you cleaned that up. You know how sensitive I am about my weight."

"And I never understood why. I mean, you always had a perfect body."

Angela looked a little surprised at his comment. From what she remembered of Marcus during those days, he was involved with so many other pretty women on campus that he never paid her any attention. "I didn't know you looked at me that way," she said, and paused, but quickly smiled and said, "Anyway, I'm glad you cleaned that up. I'd hate to have to hurt you before you get a chance to catch up, Mr. Big-Time Lawyer. I am so proud of you, Marcus. I always knew you would make it. I used to watch you on the news at night, you know, for the Ferguson trial, and I was thinking, yeah, one of us really made it big."

"That's another thing, Angela. If you've been here that long, how come I have to wait until you get in trouble to hear from you?"

"I know, I know. I didn't even know you were here when I moved to Atlanta to take this job. I didn't know until I saw you on the news. I was going to try to get in touch with you, but I knew you were busy with the trial, and I didn't think you'd even remember me."

"Are you kidding? As close as we were back then, of course I remember you."

"That's good to know."

"What about you, what are you doing these days?"

"My official title is personal assistant to the R-and-D director at Integrated Data Systems. Which basically means that I run the department."

"Integrated, I've heard of them. In fact, I've met the owner of the company."

"Brandon Marley."

"Yes. Very nice man, but a very serious and determined businessman from what I gathered."

"Yup, that's the old man. He hasn't been well lately, so his brother, Anthony, is running the company now. How do you know Brandon?"

"Parties, fund-raisers, that type of thing."

"Hobnobbin' with the rich and powerful, huh? You go, boy." Marcus gave Angela his best boyish smile and she remembered how much she had enjoyed his smile and sense of humor. "Maybe you know my boss? His name is Robert Covey."

"No, can't say that I met him."

"He's married to Brandon's daughter, Stephanie." Angela turned away. Whether she was overreacting or not, she did call him and made him drive all the way out there; she might as well tell him. "It's Stephanie that I need to talk to you about."

"What about her?"

"Somebody murdered her yesterday."

Chapter 2

Angela made Arnold Palmers, a soft drink made with lemonade and iced tea, and she and Marcus went out on the deck to talk.

"I love this spot," Angela said, looking at the sun setting.

"Your view is breathtaking." *Like you*, Marcus started to say, but didn't as Angela handed him his glass and sat down next to him. He had never told Angela, or anybody else for that matter, about the feelings he had for her. Once again, Marcus reminded himself of the promise he had made to keep it strictly business with Angela. He got down to the business at hand. "Tell me what I can do to help you, Angela."

Angela told Marcus that she was in her office earlier that morning when her assistant told her that two detectives were there to see her.

"To see me?" Angela questioned at the time.

"Yes, ma'am," her assistant said, and Angela told her to show them in. She hadn't seen Robert for the day and he wasn't accepting any of her calls, which was out of character for him. Angela hoped that whatever the police wanted, it had nothing to do with Robert, but she was suspicious that it might be.

After the detectives introduced themselves, showed her their IDs, and had taken a seat, they got down to business.

"Ms. Pettybone, do you know a woman named Stephanie Covey?"

"Yes, I do. She's my boss Robert Covey's wife."

"Could you describe the nature of your relationship with Mrs. Covey?"

Angela paused and thought about how she could answer. She understood that if the police were in her office asking about Stephanie Covey, it couldn't be good. "As I said, Stephanie is my boss's wife. Other than that, we have no relationship."

"I understand," the detective said, and looked at his notes. "Can you tell me the last time you saw Mrs. Covey?"

"Yesterday afternoon. Robert—Mr. Covey— asked me to take some documents that he needed signed to her. So I took them to her."

"Do you know what those documents contained?"

"No. Mr. Covey didn't relay that information to me, only that he needed Mrs. Covey to sign them."

"How'd you get there?"

"My car is in the shop, so I took a cab to her apartment."

"You said that you took them to her apartment."

"That's correct."

"Do you know why Mrs. Covey maintained a separate residence from her husband?"

"Mr. and Mrs. Covey are separated. To my knowledge she moved out two months ago and filed for divorce."

"You said that you didn't know the contents of the documents you were asked to get signed. Could they have anything to do with their divorce?"

"It's possible, but as I said, Mr. Covey didn't relay that information to me."

"What happened when you gave her the documents?"

"She took the envelope from me and excused herself and went to another room. I imagine she wanted to review the documents in private."

"How long was she gone?"

"No more than ten minutes."

"What was her mood when she came back?"

"If you're asking me if something she read in those documents upset her, then the answer is no. When she came out of the room and returned the documents to me, Mrs. Covey's demeanor hadn't changed."

"Did she sign the documents?"

"I didn't witness her signing them, but I assumed that she had. Mrs. Covey didn't say anything to make me think that she hadn't."

"What did you do after that?"

"Mrs. Covey and I chatted for a minute or two."

"What did the two of you talk about?"

"It was nothing major, the weather. I told her

about my car being in the shop and that I had a cab waiting and then I left and went home."

"How long were you there?"

"The whole thing couldn't have taken more than fifteen minutes."

"Do you have any idea where Mr. Covey is now?"

"No, I haven't spoken with him today. His car was here when I got here this morning, but I haven't seen him."

"What time did you get here?"

"At seven thirty."

"You said that Mr. Covey's car was here when you got here, but you haven't seen or spoken with him."

"That's correct."

"Is that unusual for you not to hear from him?"

"In fact, it is. Mr. Covey and I usually have a briefing in his office at nine every morning. If he's not in town, or can't make it to the office for any reason, he always calls," Angela told the detectives, and then her curiosity could take no more. "Would you mind telling me what this is about?"

"Mrs. Covey was murdered yesterday afternoon."

"Oh my goodness."

"To our knowledge, you were the last one to see her alive. When you were leaving the building, did you see anything or anybody out of the ordinary?"

"No, I didn't," Angela replied, but her mind hadn't gotten past *you were the last one to see her alive*.

"Thank you for your time, Ms. Pettybone. If you think of anything that might be helpful please give me a call," he said, and handed her a card. "And if you see or hear from Mr. Covey, please ask him to give me a call," the detective added, and then they stood up. "We'll be in touch. I may have some more questions for you."

After the detectives left, Angela tried to call Robert Covey, but once again, he did not answer. Angela returned the phone to its cradle and considered the worst. Had Robert murdered Stephanie? Was he even capable of such a thing? The Robert she knew was a nice and gentle man. But there were so many things going on, things that Robert hadn't chosen to tell her about, and he'd been acting so strange lately. She couldn't be sure.

"I was so shaken up that I called you. Then I cleared my schedule and I took the rest of the day off," Angela told Marcus.

"Did you kill her?" Marcus asked. It was a question that he never used to ask his clients; Panthea Daniels changed all that for him. Which wasn't any big deal; they all said they didn't do it anyway. But Marcus felt that everybody had a right to legal defense, even the ones that are guilty. But it was a question he was asking more and more lately.

"No," Angela said quickly, but definitely. She was a little put out that he would even have to ask her that. But then she remembered that they were strangers now. It had been fifteen years since they'd seen each other. People change.

"Then based on what you just told me, you have nothing to worry about. The detectives seemed more interested in the nature of the relationship between Mr. and Mrs. Covey, the contents of those documents, and the whereabouts of your boss. I don't see any problems for you. Unless there's more."

"There's more."

"There always is. Why don't you start at the beginning?"

Angela looked at Marcus and thought about how much she wanted to tell him. How much more he needed to know. "After graduation, I moved to Denver and got a job working as an associate project manager for a software company. I moved here to take this position. It was more money, and I always liked Atlanta since you, me, and Darnel used to come here while we were in college, remember?"

"I remember those days. I fell in love with this city back then too. We had a lot of good times here."

"We always had fun together." Angela smiled as memories of those days rolled through her mind, and Marcus wondered if any of those memories were about him. "Anyway, I moved here and went to work for Robert. He was handsome, intelligent, driven, charismatic, and very charming," she said, and Marcus watched Angela's face come to life.

"And very married," Marcus said dryly.

"Very. But that didn't stop me from falling in love with him."

"So you were having an affair with him?" Marcus asked in a voice that Angela took as moral disapproval of her relationship with Robert, but was actually jealousy, and he wondered why.

For some reason, having Marcus's approval of her

seemed very important to Angela. "I'm ashamed to admit it to you, but yes. It didn't happen right away. It began about a year and a half ago, I guess. It wasn't something I planned, it just happened."

"Is that why they were divorcing?" Marcus asked quickly, because he didn't want to hear any more details.

"Partly. They had a number of issues before I came along, believe me. She found out that he was seeing somebody and that was just the last straw."

"Did she know it was you that Robert was seeing?"

"Robert said she knew he was seeing somebody, but he was sure that she didn't know who it was."

"Did you kill her?" Marcus asked again.

"No," Angela said with her pretty face twisted in disbelief that Marcus felt the need to ask her again.

"Do you think Robert killed her?"

"I don't know," Angela said, and looked away.

Marcus wasn't sure what to read into that look, but it was something. "I know what you told the police, but do you know what was in those papers?"

"He didn't tell me, but I know that they are liquidating some of their assets. He needed her permission to do so. I just assumed that that's what they were."

"If the two of you were having an affair, why would he send you to get his estranged wife to sign papers? Especially since you are the reason they are estranged"

"That's the way it's always been. If I stopped

having contact with her once the affair began, that might have sent up red flags."

"And when you saw her that day did she give you any indication that she knew it was you Robert was involved with?"

"Not at all. She was her usual above-it-all, diva-licious self," Angela said, and laughed the laugh that Marcus had loved to hear all those years ago.

"Would you like another glass?" Angela asked, noticing that his glass was empty.

"Thank you." He handed her the glass and watched her as she walked away. Angela's laugh was the first thing he fell in love with.

He thought back to the first time he saw her walking across campus. And then she turned around. When Marcus saw her face he was hooked. It was love at first sight. There was an energy between them. But instead of going after her, Marcus lay back, calling himself waiting on her to make the first move. While he was lying back waiting on her, Darnel was all over her. Now here they were again. Fate had seemingly presented him with a second chance, and Darnel was nowhere in sight.

While she was in the kitchen, memories of those days raced through Angela's mind. Although she was dating Darnel, she and Marcus had spent a lot of time together. They had a lot in common, and they used to talk. They'd talk for hours about nothing in particular. Darnel never was much of a talker, but he was very good at expressing himself in other ways.

She always thought that Marcus was fine, but

thought he was too much of a womanizer for her taste. Marcus used to tell her that he was just waiting for the right woman to come along and she would put a stop to his days of chasing *every woman on campus*, Angela thought, and smiled. But in spite of that, Marcus always treated her with respect, more respect than most men had. She wondered if the right woman ever came along for him. Angela hadn't noticed a ring on his finger, so she assumed that he never did find the one he was looking for. Never knowing that she was the one he was talking about.

When Angela came back and handed Marcus his glass, she sat down next to him. The two old friends sat quietly watching the view.

"So, have you heard from Darnel?" Marcus asked.

"I saw him about five years ago. I was in Oakland on a business trip."

"The last time we spoke he said he was going to the Bay Area. How's he doing?"

Angela looked at Marcus and shook her head.

"That bad?"

"He didn't look good. When I saw him he was begging for change outside the hotel I was staying at."

"Did you talk to him?"

"No, I couldn't. I dated the guy for almost four years and now look at us. What would I say to him? 'How you doing?'" Angela asked facetiously. "It was pretty obvious how he was doing. I got in my cab quickly and asked the driver to give him twenty dollars. What else could I do?"

"Nothing, I guess. Damn, sorry to hear that

about Darnel. He had such big plans for himself when he went out there. The last few times I talked to him, he said things were going great. Then we lost touch."

"How did we lose touch with each other, Marcus?"

"I believe you moved to Denver and never called."

"Call you where? Darnel said you didn't have a phone."

Marcus laughed. "He told me you didn't have a phone," he said, and remembered how mad Darnel used to get anytime he asked about getting in touch with Angela. After a while he stopped asking for the sake of the friendship.

"You don't think Darnel was jealous of us all those years and never said anything?"

"No," Marcus lied. It was always obvious to him that Darnel was jealous, if not suspicious, of their friendship, and wondered how Angela never saw it. *I guess you only see what you want to see.*

Chapter 3

"So, what about you, Marcus?"

"What about me?"

"I don't see a ring on that finger. I guess you never found that right woman?"

"Yes, I did. And I married and divorced her. I caught her in bed with another man."

"I'm sorry to hear that," Angela said, and felt bad for asking.

"I was sorry to see it," Marcus said nonchalantly. "And you. The beautiful Angela Pettybone. How come some very lucky man hasn't put a ring on our finger?"

"Two things. Never found the time. Never found the man. When I got to Denver I was too caught up in work to make a relationship work. You men—that's not fair, some men have a problem with a career-minded woman." Angela thought that maybe that was why it was so easy for her to fall for Robert. With him, she could have the best of both worlds.

"Why Denver?"

"Wanted to get out of New York. Get away from Darnel if I wanted to be honest."

"I always wondered why he didn't go out there with you and he never said." *What he said was she'd be back*, Marcus remembered him saying.

"It wasn't that he didn't want to. I just realized that Darnel and I were going in different directions. I knew what I wanted to do."

"You always did."

"He never did know what he wanted. It was always take it as it comes."

"That's what he used to say."

"Well, that wasn't enough for me. I knew it never would be and that he would never change. I want a man who knows what he wants and goes after it." Angela looked at Marcus. "Maybe I chose the wrong guy?"

"Maybe you did," Marcus said, and felt the vibration of his phone in his pocket. He pulled it out and looked at the display. "Excuse me, Angela. I need to take this call," he said before pressing the Talk button. "Yes, Janise?"

"You're not going to believe this, but Judge Joseph's clerk called to say that he is going to rule on your motions in the Nadia Whitfield case."

Marcus glanced at his watch. "You're kidding. At this hour, he's ready to make a ruling?"

"In thirty minutes."

"I'm on my way," Marcus told Janise, and pressed END. He turned to Angela. "I'm sorry, but I have to go now. A judge is ready to rule on my motions and

I need to be there in thirty minutes. Like I said, I don't think you have anything to worry about." Marcus stood up and started for the door.

"That's good to know," Angela said, and walked Marcus to the door.

"But let's get together tomorrow. If nothing else, it will give us a chance to talk some more."

"I'd like that." Angela smiled, and Marcus felt himself getting a little weak for her all over again.

"I'll call you."

"See that you do," Angela said, and hugged Marcus.

"Good night, Angela."

"See you tomorrow," she said, and closed the door, knowing that she had a lot more that she needed to tell him. Angela was in deep with Robert. She was sure that he was involved in something. Angela couldn't help but wonder if it was that something that got Stephanie Covey murdered.

Marcus got in his car and drove as fast as traffic would allow downtown to the Fulton County Courthouse. He had filed a motion for his client, Nadia Whitfield, to be tried separately for an attempted bank robbery. It was his belief that if she were tried alone she would probably not be found guilty of any felony murder. However, if she were tried along with Calvin Slinger, the only other surviving member of gang, Nadia would most certainly be found guilty.

His motion was based on logic, and supported by precedence. "Your Honor, Nadia Whitfield was un-armed and had surrendered to authorities and was in police custody before any violence occurred inside the bank."

Assistant District Attorney Izella Hawkins didn't offer much resistance to the motion, and the judge was sympathetic to his argument, granted the motion, and set a date for the trial to begin in a month.

"Let's talk on Monday, Marcus," Izella said as they left the judge's chambers.

"No problem, what are we going to talk about?"

Izella stopped in her tracks and put her hand on her hip. "I know you're not thinking about going to trial with this."

"No," Marcus said, and kept walking. "But on Monday I plan on filing a motion to dismiss the robbery charge."

"On what grounds?"

Marcus stopped and walked back to Izella. "I take it you don't want to wait until Tuesday to read my motion?"

"Stop playing with me, Marcus."

"Ask the first officers on the scene if they read Ms. Whitfield her rights. If they did, it's not in either of their statements."

"Of course they did."

"No, actually they didn't," Marcus said, and started walking. "When Ms. Whitfield saw the police, she immediately put up her hands. They cuffed her, put her in the car, and entered the bank. That's what their statements say."

"It's in the arresting officer's statement," Izella said confidently.

"His statement says that he Mirandized Calvin Slinger and placed him in the vehicle with the other suspect. Nobody read Ms. Whitfield her rights. That makes any statements she made inadmissible."

Izella looked at Marcus and thought for a second. "Wait a minute, Marcus. You could have gotten the murder charges dismissed on the same grounds."

"I know that, Izella. I am a lawyer, you know."

"Then why aren't you?"

"When I explained to Ms. Whitfield that I could get the murder charges dismissed, she said that's not what she wanted to do. She said that she broke the law and should stand trial for it."

"You're kidding."

"No, I'm not. Ms. Whitfield found God since she's been in her cell."

"Oh Lord."

"Exactly. Once the robbery charge is dismissed, that will just leave the murder charge. Do you think a jury will convict her of a murder that was committed while she was in police custody?"

"They might," Izella said sheepishly.

"Not if you can't connect her to the robbery, and since all of her statements about the robbery will be inadmissible, I plan on objecting every time you attempt it. So why don't we talk about a plea on Wednesday?"

"You know, Marcus, this is exactly why I hate you. Talk to you Wednesday," Izella said as she and Marcus got on the elevator.

When Marcus got back to his office, Garrett Mason was waiting for him. He was a private investigator that Marcus used on murder cases. Garrett used to work for the City of Atlanta Police Department, but he got caught up in a corruption scandal. Marcus defended him and he was eventually cleared of the charges, but the damage was done. He quit the force and went into business for himself as a private investigator. Over the years, Garrett and Marcus had become friends.

"Sorry I'm late, Garrett. Judge Joseph just ruled on a motion."

"Yeah. Janise told me before she left me waiting here. How did it go?"

"He ruled in my favor."

"Good. So, what's next? Child support is expensive." Garrett was recently divorced from his wife, Paven. Now he was paying a healthy amount of child support for their three children.

"How are the kids?" Marcus asked, and sat down at his desk.

"Weren't you listening? They're expensive. On top of what I gotta give Paven every month, every time I turn around one of the kids is callin' me with 'Daddy, I need this, Daddy, I need that.' So I hope you called me down here for some work, and I hope the job lasts a long time."

"Paven still hasn't found a job yet?"

"Nope. She can't find what she ain't lookin' for. And why should she? She's getting a chunk of money. The cars are paid for, I still pay for the house and all the bills."

"That one was your idea," Marcus added quickly, while he loosened his tie.

"Irrelevant."

"I'm just saying that it was you beating his chest, insisting that you would take care of the mortgage and all the bills."

"You could have objected."

"I thought that's what I was doing when I said what Mr. Mason means, and what you said is, 'He'll take care of the bills.'"

"Irrelevant."

"What is relevant?"

"That I need work. So, what you got?"

"Stephanie Covey. Murdered yesterday."

"Whose jurisdiction was it in?" Garrett asked.

"All I can tell is that it's in Cobb County."

"So it could be Cobb County PD or Marietta PD." Garrett made notes while he talked. "Who's the client?"

"The victim's husband's personal assistant, Angela Pettybone. We were friends in college. And before you ask, just friends." Marcus didn't think that Garrett needed to know that he had a schoolboy crush on her.

"Is she pretty?"

"Yes, she is. Very. A little heavier, but she looks just like she did in college."

"Marcus."

"Yes."

"Don't fuck her."

"I don't fuck all my clients."

"No, just the pretty ones."

"Nadia's pretty, I didn't fuck her."

"No. No, you didn't. But you can't really count her since she was denied bail."

"Irrelevant and immaterial."

"Whatever. What you got on this Stephanie Covey?"

"Not much. Just the address of the crime scene."

"What's your girl saying?"

"Angela said that she went to see her to drop off some papers to be signed. Once she got them signed, she left and Mrs. Covey was alive."

"What the cops talkin' 'bout?"

"They questioned her this morning in her office. But from what she told me of the interview, they were more concerned with her husband's whereabouts."

"His name?"

"Robert Covey. He's R-and-D director for Integrated Data Systems. See what you can find out about the murder, and start looking at Robert and Angela."

"Whoa, whoa, slow down. Don't you mean Robert and Stephanie?"

"No. I meant Robert and Angela. Did I forget to mention that she was having an affair with Robert?"

"Yeah, you did. But now I know why you ain't trying to fuck her. But anyway, that does complicate things."

"I want to know early on if she's going to get dragged into the murder by the affair. So let's get out in front of this."

"I'm on it," Garrett said, and got up to leave.

"I'm right behind you, Garrett." Marcus turned off his computer and followed Garrett out of the office.

On the way home, Marcus thought about Angela. In spite of his promise to himself, he couldn't seem to get her off his mind. Back in college, he had fallen in love with her when he first saw her, but it was the sound of her voice that pulled him over the edge. He could sit and talk to Angela and gaze at her beauty for hours and never tire.

When he got to his house, Marcus pulled into the driveway and put the car in park. He got out of the car and began walking toward the house. As he got closer, Marcus could see that the front door was open.

Wide open.

Knowing that he had closed and locked the door when he left that morning, Marcus returned to his vehicle and called the police from his cell phone.

Chapter 4

Since Marcus lived in a nice neighborhood, the Dekalb County police got to his house in seven minutes. After Marcus explained that when he got home he found his front door open, the responding officer went inside and checked the house.

When the officer came out of the house, he approached Marcus. "I checked the entire residence, sir, and I didn't find anybody or anything that appeared out of the ordinary. There is no sign of forced entry."

"I understand."

"What I would like to do now is for you and me to walk through the residence to determine if anything is missing or has been disturbed. But I have to ask you to please not touch anything."

Marcus followed the officer into the house, knowing without having to be told the importance of preserving the potential crime scene.

Once the two had walked through the house and determined that nothing was missing or seemed to have been disturbed, they came back outside and the officer began filling out his report. "May have just been some kids playing a prank." The officer handed Marcus his card. "Give me a call if you have any more problems."

"Thank you, Officer."

The officer left, and left Marcus with something to think about. He was more than sure that he had closed the door before he left the house that morning. If that was the case, someone, for some reason, broke into his house. And if that was the case, why go through all the trouble of breaking into the house and not take anything?

Had he come home in time to scare the would-be robbers off? And what about the alarm?

The only people who knew his alarm code were his personal assistant, Janise, and Garrett, whom he had just left. Surely if Garrett had reason to be in the house, he would have mentioned it. And besides, even if one of them had been in the house, Marcus was sure that neither of them would leave the door open.

That left two possibilities: either somebody or a group of somebodys broke in to rob the place, or somebody had a key and his alarm code. Marcus smiled briefly and thought that maybe it was Carmen. She had both a key and knew the alarm code, but she was in Europe.

There was the possibility that she was in town and wanted to surprise him. She could have let herself in, seen him driving up, opened the door, and hidden. "That would be just like her," Marcus said aloud as he walked to the bar to pour himself a glass of Hennessey. But then he reasoned that if that was the case, the officer would have walked Carmen out in handcuffs and they would have had a good laugh about it.

Since he was sure that Carmen wouldn't leave the door open if she wasn't there, Marcus knew it wasn't her either. But the remote possibility did exist. He looked at his watch and thought about calling her. "Let's see, if it's seven twenty-one in Atlanta, then it's one twenty-one in the morning in Paris."

In spite of that, Marcus picked up the phone and dialed Carmen's cell number. Naturally, she was asleep when he called. "You do know what time it is, right?" asked a sleepy Carmen.

"I'm sorry to wake you up, Carmen, but you are in Paris now, aren't you?"

"Where else would I be?"

After Marcus explained the reason for the early morning call and what he hoped had happened, Carmen understood the need to call.

"I'll let you go back to sleep, Carmen. I'm sorry I woke you."

"I'm up now, and we haven't talked in a while, so talk to me, Marcus. What's up with you these days?"

When Carmen went back to Europe, at first, they talked every day. Since there was a six-hour time difference, Carmen had to set her alarm for 5:00 A.M. so she could catch Marcus in bed. She said it was a way for them to be in bed together. They would spend hours talking until either Marcus fell asleep or she had to get up. But when Carmen started getting more work as a model, and shoots began early, her calls became less frequent and were never as long.

They had continued to speak every day, but by then calls consisted of a rundown of their day and plans to talk later, and then they would both hang up, getting back to their separate lives.

For the next couple of hours, Marcus and Carmen caught up on each other's lives. They had gotten to the point in their relationship where they agreed to be just friends, as long as they weren't on the same continent. However, if a time ever came in their lives that they were in the same place, at the same time, then all bets were off.

"You belong to me, Marcus Douglas," Carmen told him.

The two friends talked for a while, and then the conversation returned to his break-in.

"You know who I think it is?" Carmen asked.

"Who?"

"That woman you told me about. What was her name again?"

"Panthea Daniels."

Marcus had told Carmen about his experience with Panthea, after it was over of course. While it was going on, Marcus never mentioned it and never evaded the question nor made up some excuse to get off the phone anytime Carmen would ask a question like, "So, is there anybody new in your life that I need to know about?"

Marcus sat back in his chair and thought for a second. "I haven't even thought about it being her."

"You're not still seeing her, are you?" Carmen

asked with more of an attitude than a friend should have.

"I'm not. I haven't seen or heard from Panthea in more than two months. I don't think it's her; at least I hope it's not her. It's probably just what the cop said. Some kids playing a prank."

"For your sake, I hope you're right. A woman like her is capable of anything." Carmen yawned. "Well, my dear, I'm getting sleepy again. Probably because it's after three in the morning here."

"Like I said, I'm sorry I woke you. But I am glad we got a chance to talk. I enjoyed it."

"Yeah, I am good company."

"Always were."

"We really should do this more often."

"You're right, we should. I promise to call more often."

"Me too. You take care of yourself, Marcus, okay? Promise me you'll be careful."

"I promise."

"And stay away from that crazy woman," Carmen laughed. "You know, if you were saving it for me like I'm saving it for you, you wouldn't have whipped that whatever her name is, and none of this would be happening."

"Are you really saving it for me, Carmen?"

"Yes."

"Really?"

"But there are two reasons for that. One is that I'm not seeing anybody now, and haven't for a while. And the other is that I love you, Marcus, and that contributes to the first reason."

"I love you too, Carmen."

"I know you do, but you don't have to say it just because I did."

"I'm not. I love you."

"Good. Because you still belong to me, Marcus Douglas. And to be honest with you, I have been thinking a lot lately about coming back to the States."

"Don't play with me, Carmen."

"I'm not. I was thinking New York or maybe even L.A., but I'm leaning toward New York."

"New York, huh? I may just have to open an office there."

"Are you trying to sweeten the deal?"

"Absolutely. I'd offer you money if I thought it would do any good. Come home. I love you and we belong together."

"Good night, Marcus." Carmen yawned.

"Good night, Carmen. We'll talk soon."

After hanging up with Carmen, Marcus thought about the possibility of Carmen coming back to America. Though the idea excited him, it wasn't long before his mind turned to the possibility that it might be Panthea that broke into his house. She was the most logical candidate, but one he hadn't even considered.

While she was his client, Marcus thought it was best that they not be seen around the city together. And coming to his house was out of the question. But there were two times when Panthea did come to the house.

The first time they got together, they were on

their way to Savannah for the weekend, when Marcus realized that he had forgotten something.

"I'll just be a minute," Marcus said when they pulled into the driveway that day.

"Can I see the house? I think how a man decorates his house says a lot about him."

At the time, Marcus thought it was cute. "Okay," he said, and laughed a little. "Come on."

Panthea could then have seen him enter the code and remembered it. That would explain the alarm, but the officer said there was no sign of forced entry. They had spent a lot of time together, so she could easily have made a copy of his key.

For months after Marcus ended their relationship, Panthea had tried to get Marcus to see her. She'd call him every night when he got home. Panthea would plead her case, reminding him of how he said he felt about her and how she still felt about him. How they had found something special in each other; something that was too strong to just give up on. She would tempt him with her sexuality, and her point was always the same. "If I could just see you, baby."

When begging on the phone didn't work, Panthea stepped up her tactics. She began showing up at places where he'd be. He thought back to one time when he was having dinner at Pittypat's Porch, a restaurant that specialized in southern cuisine, which wasn't far from his office, discussing a case with Tiffanie Powers.

Tiffanie was the best lawyer in his office, and Marcus had been giving serious consideration to making her a partner in the firm. But on that particular night, they had been working late on a trial brief to resolve a disputed point of evidence in a case that Tiffanie was working on. They had finished their meal, and Marcus was about to call for the check when Panthea sat down at the table.

"Hello, Tiffanie," Panthea said quickly, and turned to Marcus.

He looked at her with fire in his eyes. "What are you doing here?"

"Why don't you answer the phone or return any of my calls, Marcus? How can you just ignore me like this?"

"I think I should be going," Tiffanie said, and began gathering her things. Marcus had mentioned that he was having what he called *issues* with Panthea and she wanted no part of it.

"Good night, Tiffanie," Panthea said without looking at her. "It is just so disrespectful for you to just ignore me."

"I'm sorry about this, Tiffanie," Marcus said. He too wasn't looking at Tiffanie when he spoke. His eyes were locked on Panthea's.

"He's not sorry, Tiffanie. He doesn't care about you or how you feel. Marcus doesn't care about anybody but himself," Panthea spat out.

"We'll talk in the morning." Tiffanie stood up and motioned for Marcus to call her, before she walked out of the restaurant.

"What are you doing here?" Marcus asked as Panthea signaled for a waiter.

"You won't talk to me."

"What is there for us to talk about?"

"We have a lot to talk about, Marcus, and you know it," Panthea said as the waiter stepped to the table. "I'll have a glass of Chardonnay, and bring him whatever he's drinking."

"No. Bring the lady her wine, and bring me the check," Marcus said angrily, and the waiter scurried away from the table.

"There is nothing for us to talk about, Panthea. Why can't you understand that it's over between us?"

"What I don't understand is why it's over. Maybe if I understood that I could accept it. But I just can't for the life of me understand why. And I have tried, tried to understand why you could not want for us to be together."

"We have been over this so many times, Panthea. I don't know if I'll ever be able to trust you."

"It would take time. All we need is time, baby. Time together. Not with you ignoring me—when we're together. In time you will see that I'm not that person anymore. That person died that night in Houston."

"How would I ever know that?"

"You'd learn to trust me, but that is not going to happen if you keep ignoring me, Marcus."

"That's the problem, I don't trust you. How could you keep something like that from me?"

"I didn't know what you'd think of me if I told you the truth, and I couldn't take that chance."

Marcus leaned forward quickly. "You could have trusted me!" he said louder than he should in the crowded restaurant. Marcus looked around to see how many people were looking at him and lowered his voice. "I can understand your not telling your lawyer, but I was more than just your lawyer. How could you just sit there, knowing that I had people that were conducting an investigation, and you not tell me? You had to know I'd find out."

"You said you wanted to love me forever," Panthea said as if nothing Marcus said had any bearing on what she was there to talk about. "You said you wanted to wake up every morning and I would be the first thing you see when you opened your eyes. You said that we had created something special. Those were your words, Marcus. Were they all lies?"

"No. They weren't lies. Not when I said them. But all those words were based on a lie. Trust can't exist when it's built on lies."

"I haven't lied to you, Marcus. I kept something from you. That's all I did. I kept something from you that I've never told another living soul."

"That's the problem."

The waiter returned with Panthea's Chardonnay and the check. Marcus threw some money on the table and stood up. "I wasn't any other living soul."

Marcus walked out and Panthea followed quickly behind him. In stilettos and a tight skirt, it was hard for Panthea to keep up with him. She caught up with him in the parking lot.

When he'd arrived at the restaurant, the only space was one in between a van and a brick wall. Thinking that if the van was still there when he came out, it would be hard to back out, Marcus had backed the car in, and now Panthea was standing in front of it. After honking the horn and yelling for her to move, Marcus got out of the car and walked around to the front.

"This is silly, Panthea."

"No. What's silly is what you're doing. We love each other, Marcus. We should be together."

The conversation continued in much the same manner for almost an hour before Panthea changed tactics again. "Why can't you just fuck me?"

Marcus dropped his head. "I'm not going anywhere with you, Panthea."

"You don't have to. Just fuck me now and I'll leave. Otherwise, we'll be out here all night. I have nothing to do."

"No."

"You know you want me, Marcus. You know you want to feel my hands all over your body. My body against yours." Panthea stepped closer to Marcus and pressed her body against his. "You deep inside me, while I whisper my nasty thoughts in your ear. You know how you love it when I talk nasty to you."

Marcus made what amounted to a halfhearted attempt to push Panthea off him. If he wanted to be honest with himself, and right then he was trying his best not to, Marcus would have to admit that he did want her. In fact, he'd been thinking of nothing but that since she sat down at the table.

Panthea was wearing a tight black skirt because she knew how much he liked seeing her in that color. She had on a white blouse, with a plunging neckline and a string of pearls that fell into her abundant cleavage.

Panthea was hard to resist.

She always had been and tonight was no different. The more she talked and wiggled her body against his, the more he wanted to pull up that skirt, bend her over, and give her what they both wanted.

"We can't do it right here," he said.

"Why not?"

"People will see us."

"Who is going to care what we're doing? I don't care if people see me." Panthea took a step back and began gyrating her body and slowly easing up her skirt.

"Stop that."

"Why? Afraid you might see something you can't resist?"

Marcus wanted to scream, "Yes!" but instead he remained silent and watched Panthea until he could see that she wasn't wearing anything under her skirt. At that point, he couldn't take it anymore. He grabbed Panthea by the hand and literally dragged her behind the car. He opened the trunk and began unbuckling his pants. "Bend over."

But instead, Panthea stood and watched him while he pulled down his zipper. Panthea quickly took him into her mouth and when it was nice and stiff the way she liked it, she complied with his request.

Marcus grabbed her by the hips and rammed himself into Panthea's waiting wetness. While people walked by to pick up their cars, Marcus and Panthea went at it like dogs in heat. At first, Marcus was worried that the owner of the van would come, but after a while, the only thing on his mind was how wet Panthea was, and how much he missed being inside her. After they finished, they fixed their clothes and Panthea said good night and left Marcus alone in the parking lot.

Thinking about that night with Panthea made Marcus realize that she couldn't have been the one who had broken into his house. Even though they joked when they first met about her being a stalker, she wasn't that type of person. All she wanted was for Marcus to love her the way he had before. Panthea wasn't a violent person.

It was getting late so Marcus got ready to call it a night. He briefly gave some thought to calling one of his fuck buddies, *you know, just to release some tension*, but he decided against it. He got in bed and had fallen asleep, until the phone rang at two forty-five in the morning.

Marcus looked at the clock, wondering who was calling him at this hour. "Hello," he answered, still half asleep. But no one said anything. He hung up the phone and was able to drop back off to sleep without any problem.

At five o'clock, the phone rang again. Once again, Marcus answered, and once again, no one said a word.

Chapter 5

Garrett Mason was up and out of his apartment before eight o'clock that Friday morning, even though he didn't get to sleep until after four.

After he left Marcus's office, he began to look into Stephanie Covey's murder. His first task was to find out whose jurisdiction the murder was committed in. The metropolitan Atlanta area is made up of five counties, each with its own county police force. Some of the larger cities within the counties have their own city police force.

Armed with a Google map, Garrett drove out to the address he had gotten from Marcus. When he found the apartment complex, he turned in and began looking for the building. It wasn't hard to find.

Garrett slowed down when he saw a Marietta police cruiser parked in front of the building. Garrett could see an officer in the car. At that point, Garrett knew that he wouldn't get a look at the crime scene, at least not that night. But the fact that there was a cruiser parked outside intrigued him.

Garrett drove a few buildings down and got out of his car. He walked toward the building until he was out of the officer's direct line of sight. Then he waited for a few minutes before returning to his car. Garrett got back in his car and waited. He was curious to find out if the cruiser would leave. He sat there for a half hour before Garrett started his car and drove off. The cruiser didn't move.

The fact that the police had somebody literally guarding the crime scene indicated to Garrett that either it was a particularly gruesome crime scene, or the victim was somebody important.

"Or both," Garrett said aloud as he left the complex. He took out his cell phone and called Detective John Brunet. The two had been partners until Garrett got assigned to the narcotics task force and got caught up in the corruption scandal.

"Crazy John!"

"That you, Mason?"

"Who else calls you Crazy John?"

"A few people call me that once in a while. So, to what do I owe the honor of a call from the great Garrett Mason? You need somebody to hold your coat for your next TV appearance?"

"Don't hate. Besides, it was just one time."

"One time more than me."

"Whatever, John. I need a favor."

"Naturally. What you got?"

"I was trying to get a look at a crime scene a little while ago, but there's a Marietta city cruiser parked out front."

"That doesn't sound good."

"I'm sayin'."

"Who's the vic?"

"Vic's name is Stephanie Covey," Garrett told John, and gave him the address.

"I'll make some calls and get back to you."

"Thanks, John."

When Garrett still hadn't heard from John an hour and a half later, he drove by the precinct to see if he was still there. Seeing his car in the parking lot, he went in to find him. After shaking a few hands and swapping old cop stories, Garrett found John Brunet seated at his desk with the phone pressed to his ear. He motioned for Garrett to sit down while he finished his call. When he hung up the phone, John stood up and grabbed his jacket.

"Calling it a night, John?"

"Yeah, let somebody else save the world tonight. There's a tall Bud waiting for me somewhere."

"You got anything for me?"

"Walk with me."

Garrett followed John out of the building and to his car. Before he could ask John what he had for him, he said, "All I got to say is that my name is spelled B-R-U-N-E-T, that's Brunet with one *n*, not two."

"What are you talking about?"

"That case you asked me to look into, Stephanie Covey. It's big."

"Give it up, John. Gruesome or somebody?"

"Both."

"I was afraid you'd say that. What you got?"

"This Stephanie Covey is the daughter of some guy named Brandon Marley."

"Never heard of him."

"He's some big-time business tycoon. Plays golf with the governor, for Christ's sake."

"That's why the special treatment. How'd she get it?"

"That's just it. I can't get any information. I called around and they are keeping a tight lid on this one. All I can tell you is that she was shot multiple times."

After hearing that, Garrett and Brunet talked for a while before saying good night. On his way home, he thought about how much more difficult it was going to be to get information about the murder. Thinking that Marcus wanted to get out in front of it quickly, Garrett decided that he would have to do something he really didn't want to do. *I'm gonna need to call in a favor*, he thought as he went into his apartment building. When he reached the top of the steps, he was surprised to see somebody sitting on the porch in front of the door. He was about to reach for his gun when he saw it was his oldest daughter, Aleana.

"I was beginning to think you weren't coming home," Aleana said as she stood up to hug her father.

"What you doing here? Is everything all right?" Garrett asked excitedly.

"Calm down, Daddy. There's nothing wrong. I just need to talk to you."

"Must be important if it couldn't wait until I saw you guys tomorrow."

"It is," Aleana said while she stretched.

"How long have you been waiting?"

"About an hour and a half, I guess. Maybe longer."

"Why didn't you just wait in the car?"

"I didn't drive."

"Oh. How'd you get here, then?"

"I walked."

"You walked?"

"It's only three miles."

Garrett knew it must be something important for Aleana to walk all the way over there. *She hates to walk.* He unlocked the door to his small one-bedroom apartment and they went inside. After the divorce, the tiny apartment was all he could really afford.

Garrett and Paven had begun seeing each other when they were both in the ninth grade. The relationship continued when they were both accepted at the University of Georgia. During her sophomore year, Paven got pregnant with Aleana. Garrett insisted that they had to get married, and they soon were. Garrett quit school to support his new family. He worked any job he could, until he received an offer to join the Atlanta Police Department.

After Aleana was born, Paven went back to college. She was four months pregnant with Gary when she received her degree in chemistry. Now with two young children, Paven didn't want strangers raising their children. She wanted to stay home for a few years to give them a good foundation. Garrett took the first of many second jobs. Four years later, their youngest child, Monique, was born.

"Does your mother know you're here?" Garrett asked.

"No."

"You should call her, she's probably worried."

"I doubt that," Aleana said, and sat down on the couch.

Garrett sat down next to her. "What's that supposed to mean? You and your mother have a fight or something?"

"No, we didn't have a fight. At least not this week."

"Then what's the problem?"

"Mom. That's the problem."

"What do you mean, Aleana, why is your mother the problem?"

"She's never home."

"What you mean, she's never home?"

"Just what I said, Daddy. Mommy is never home. And when she is home, she's always asleep. When she gets up, it's to get ready to leave the house again."

Garrett put his arm around his daughter. "Aleana, your mother is a single woman now. She has a right to go out sometimes."

"I understand that, but she is still our mother, and she still has some responsibilities to her children."

"I think you just need to go on and tell me what you're trying to tell me."

"I already did. She is never at home. There are days at a time when none of us sees her."

"Days?"

"Yes, Daddy, days."

"That's not right."

"That's what I been trying to tell you."

"How long has this been going on?"

"Almost a year."

"A year!" Garrett was shocked. "How come I'm just hearing about this?"

"Mommy made me promise not to tell you."

"A promise you're breaking now. Why?"

"Daddy, I'm eighteen years old. This is my senior year and I can't do anything, because I always got to be home to take care of Monique."

"She told you not to tell me, huh?"

"Daddy, there's a whole lot going on in that house that you don't know about."

"Like what?"

"Did you know Gary got suspended from school?"

"For what?"

"Smokin' weed in the boys' bathroom. Mommy said she was gonna tell you."

"She never said a word about it." His face was getting tight.

"And it wasn't the first time."

"What?"

"The first two times were for fighting."

"Two times?"

"Yes! Two times."

"I did not know that," Garrett said, and dropped his head. Paven was a grown woman, and single. What she did was none of his business, but hearing that his son had been suspended from school three times upset him. It made him feel like a bad father. Something he had tried so hard to avoid.

"What you think, Gary was gonna tell you?"

"Yeah. He's always been a good kid. Something must be going on with him to be acting that way." Garrett blamed himself for not being there.

"You don't know Gary anymore. He's changed. He's a little thug now."

"Thug?"

"Yes. Pants-hangin'-off-his-behind, big-white-T-shirt, hat-turned-to-the-side kind of thug."

"He's not sellin' drugs, is he?"

"Honestly, Daddy, I don't know. He's never home either, except when you come over for the weekend."

Since Garrett's apartment was so small, it would be too small for all three children to visit at once. So when it came time for him to visit, Paven would leave and Garrett would sleep on the couch.

"Daddy, it's like this. When you come over, Gary puts a belt on and we all try to act like the good kids we were when you were living with us. Once you leave, it's back to normal."

"What about Monique?"

"She hasn't gotten suspended yet—"

"Yet?"

"Her mouth is her problem. Talkin' in class, talkin' back to her teachers. One of them called for Mommy to come to the school to talk about it, but she didn't go."

"Why not?"

"She said she had something important to do and made me go."

"You?"

"Yes, Daddy. I'm the only *responsible* adult in the house. She don't have time for stuff like that."

"What is your mother doing that she don't have time to go to school to see about Monique?"

"You tell me."

"How come this is the first I'm hearing of all this?"

"I told you, she made all of us promise not to tell you. That's why I didn't drive over here. When Mommy leaves she always takes the keys to both cars to make sure I don't go anywhere."

"Wait a minute. If your mother's not home, who's home with Monique?"

"She's alone. Come on, Dad, she's not a baby. Monique is eleven years old, she can be home for a while by herself. Mommy leaves her alone all the time."

Garrett and Alcana ended up talking until three o'clock in the morning before Garrett took her home. When he got to the house, Paven wasn't home. Garrett drove home thinking about what could be going on with his ex-wife.

On the way to the precinct the following morning, Garrett thought about how his family had fallen apart without him. He thought back to the day that Paven told him she was leaving him and taking the children to live with her mother. "What you mean, you leavin' me, Paven?"

"I can't say it any plainer than that. I'm not happy with us, Garrett."

"Why?"

"You're never here, for one."

"I have to work, Paven. You know there aren't any set hours in what I do. I gotta work to make a good life for you and the kids."

"I know that, Garrett. But do you ever think about what that is doin' to us? To your children?

We need you here with us sometimes too. They need their father."

While they were married, Garrett always had the mentality that, as long as the bills were paid, then everything was all good. So he worked. It was all he knew to do, but that wasn't enough for Paven. She told him that she felt like a prisoner in their house and a slave to the children. She said she needed some time away from Garrett, time away from their house to think about what she wanted to do. "I need to do something for myself. I don't do anything for me."

As he pulled into the precinct parking lot, Garrett remembered Paven telling him that night that she needed to know that he wanted to be a part of their children's lives. Now it seemed like it was him that needed to know that she wanted to be part of their children's lives. Something had to be done to turn his family around, and it would begin that night when Garrett went to their house to visit for the weekend.

But now he walked into the precinct to do something that he really didn't want to do. In order to get the information that he needed on Stephanie Covey, he had to ask Lieutenant Stevenson for a favor. Before he got inside the building, his cell phone rang.

"Talk to me."

"Morning, Garrett. It's Marcus."

"How's it going, Marcus?"

"I'm a little tired, but I'll live. Where are you?"

"I was just about to see if I can get some information about Stephanie Covey. But there's something else. I don't know why, but Marietta PD is keeping a tight lid on this one. My usual source can't get anything from anybody. And when I drove by the crime scene last night there was a cruiser parked outside."

"Keep me posted, Garrett."

"I will."

"There's something else I need you to do for me."

"Call it."

"I need you to find out where Panthea Daniels is."

"Panthea Daniels? I thought you stopped seeing her."

"I did. I just need to know where she is. I gotta take this call, but we'll talk later."

"You got it." Garrett ended the call and went inside and approached the desk sergeant, wondering what that was all about.

"Is the lieutenant in?" Garrett asked the desk sergeant.

"Yup. You can go on back, Mason. I know how much the lieutenant loves to see you," the sergeant laughed.

"Thanks. *Asshole*," Garrett said quietly, and made his way back to Lieutenant Stevenson's office. When he got to the office, the lieutenant was seated behind his desk, reading over a report.

Garrett stuck his head in. "Got a minute?"

Stevenson looked up. "I got all the time in the world for police business. What do you want, Mason?"

Garrett came in and sat down. Seeing the surly look on Stevenson's face, he decided to dispense with the small talk. "I need a favor."

Stevenson tipped his head to one side and looked at his watch. "Where's my calendar? I wanna note the date and time."

"Huh?"

"You, askin' me for a favor. This must be something big."

"I don't know. Brunet can't get any information."

"That's why you came to me. What's this, some big media circus for Douglas?"

"Like I said, I don't know."

"Well, I'm not a mind reader. Tell me what you got."

Garrett explained to his old lieutenant what he knew about Stephanie Covey's murder. Then he spent the next hour sitting quietly while Stevenson called around and tried to get information. When he hung up the phone, Stevenson looked very frustrated.

"What?" Garrett asked.

"I can't get anything either. All I could get was that she was shot multiple times—"

"I got that from Brunet."

"And the place was ransacked."

"That, he didn't tell me."

"Something else I know he missed."

"What's that?"

"The FBI is involved in the investigation."

Chapter 6

That Friday morning, Marcus was in the office before eight and out by noon. He had accepted an invitation to have lunch with Angela at her home. After hearing from Garrett that Marietta police weren't talking, Marcus was anxious to talk to Angela some more about the murder of Stephanie Covey, and to see her as well.

Angela served shrimp scampi, wild rice, and mixed vegetables. Everything was delicious. After lunch, the pair moved to the living room to talk about her situation.

"Have you heard from your boss yet?"

"Nothing, and I'm starting to worry about him," Angela said, and Marcus could see the pain that she was in, so he changed the topic without changing the subject.

"What exactly do you guys do at Integrated Data Systems?"

"We are a software development company that

specializes in designing custom software with the full cooperation of the client."

"What do you mean by that?"

"Our team accomplishes this by emphasizing the role that the client plays in the development process, by offering comprehensive, easily accessible information."

"You sound like the company spokesperson," Marcus laughed.

"Shhh, it's part of my presentation. Now, where was I?" Angela giggled. "Oh yeah. Basically, the developers literally become a part of their staff until the project is complete. Our goal is to increase each client's productivity and decrease the costs of the operation by helping them target and eliminate areas of inefficiency."

"So they develop software for business applications?"

"Primarily. The company started out specializing in solving specific tasks concerning application development and Web programming for various platforms. We grew from there, gradually gaining experience and recognition amongst clients and top developers, and now we've become a leader in the market of outsourced programming and development. But recently we've been doing a lot of work for the government."

"Really? What type?"

"I can't really get into the specifics of the types of contracts, Marcus. You understand, don't you?"

"I understand completely. Probably all very top secret, national-security-type stuff."

"I don't know about all that," Angela laughed, even though a number of their contracts dealt with national security. "But I can tell you that once we were awarded the contract, all Integrated employees had to apply for security clearance."

"Interesting."

"What is?"

"When my investigator tried to get information about Stephanie Covey's murder, he hit a brick wall. Now I'm thinking that it might have something to do with your company's government contracts."

"It's possible. But what's more likely is that her father is a very private man and wanted to keep it out of the press. Mr. Marley is pretty connected to several politicians."

"Yes. As I recall, he's a big contributor to the conservative wing of his party."

"How do you think we got those big government contracts? It helps when you have lunch regularly with a senator."

"Which one?"

"Jack Rambliss."

"Isn't he on the Armed Services Committee?"

"You know your politics," Angela said as the doorbell rang. She excused herself and went to answer it. When Angela opened the door, there were two men standing there.

"Good afternoon, ma'am. Detectives Pryor and Wiggins, with the Gwinnett County Police. You remember we spoke last week," the man said in a deep, southern accent as they flashed their badges.

"Yes, Detective, I remember you."

"We'd like to ask you a few questions. I promise not to take up too much of your time. May we come in?"

"Please," Angela said, and extended her arm graciously. Detective Pryor was the last person she wanted to see right now. She thought that matter was behind her, but his presence at the door meant that it wasn't. "Come in."

Angela led the detectives into the living room, where Marcus was waiting. He stood up when the detectives came into the room. He could tell by the look on her face that Angela was nervous.

"Oh. I'm sorry, ma'am. I didn't know you had company. We could come back if this is a bad time."

"No, not at all. Detectives, this is my attorney, Marcus Douglas." He shook hands with the detectives.

"Lawyer, huh?" Pryor said, and frowned. "Well, as I was telling your client, we just have a few things we need to clear up about the statement she made the first time she was interviewed."

"I understand."

Once everyone had taken his or her seats, Detective Pryor began his questioning. "I wanted to ask you about the night Floyd Dorsey was murdered."

"Floyd Dorsey?" Marcus asked in surprise, and looked at Angela, who was doing her best not to look in Marcus's direction. He had been thinking that the detectives had more questions about Stephanie Covey. But this was something else; something that made Angela nervous.

"That's right. Is there a problem?"

"No," Marcus lied. He had come to have lunch and talk about Stephanie Covey. Angela hadn't mentioned that she had been questioned in another murder. Angela should have told him about this. "I just wanted to make sure I had the name right. Go on."

"I know we've covered this before, Ms. Pettybone, but if you don't mind, could you tell us how you were acquainted with the deceased?"

"As I told you," Angela started with a bit of bite, but quickly returned to her usual professional manner. "Mr. Dorsey was a business associate of my boss, Robert Covey."

"And there was no other relationship, say of a more personal nature, that existed between you and Mr. Dorsey?"

"No. As I said, it was purely a business relationship, Detective."

"I see. Now, on the day of the murder, Mr. Covey was the last appointment Mr. Dorsey had that day. Did Mr. Covey keep the appointment?"

"No. As I explained before, at the last minute Mr. Covey was called away. So I went in his place."

"Did he tell you what was so important for him not to keep his appointment?"

"Mr. Covey didn't share that with me."

"Can you tell me what the appointment with Mr. Dorsey was about?"

"Mr. Dorsey was in negotiations with Mr. Covey for a project that our two companies would joint-venture on."

"Can you tell me what that project was about?"

Angela looked at Marcus. "Due to the sensitive nature of the project, I'll have to ask my client not to answer that question at this time. However, should the information be deemed critical to your investigation, my client would gladly answer that question, in the appropriate setting, of course," he said.

Pryor looked at Marcus and rolled his eyes. "Of course." He returned his attention to Angela. "All right, Ms. Pettybone, you said that Mr. Covey didn't share with you what the appointment was about, just that they were gonna talk about some joint venture. So if that was the case, what purpose did it serve by you keepin' the appointment for him?"

"At that point, it became a courtesy visit to say, of course, that Mr. Covey wouldn't be able to attend, and to see if there was anything that I could do, or questions I could answer about the company and our processes."

Marcus observed Angela while she answered the detectives' questions. It was obvious to him that Angela was nervous, but that was only because he knew her. What she displayed to the detectives was confidence and poise. Marcus could tell from that that Angela was good at her job, and worked well under pressure.

"Company processes, you say?" Pryor asked smugly.

"That's correct."

"What did you and Mr. Dorsey argue about?"

"We didn't argue."

"At no time during your appointment with Mr.

Dorsey did you yell?" Pryor looked down at his notes. "'Stop this. Stop this, right now.' You didn't yell that at Mr. Dorsey?"

"Not that I can recall."

"You don't remember saying, 'Stop this. Stop this right now'?"

"As I said, I don't recall saying those words."

"Is there a point to this, Detective?" Marcus interrupted. He didn't like the way this interview was going at all.

Pryor turned his icy glare at Marcus. He could tell by his look that Pryor had no use for lawyers. "As I said, I just wanna be clear about some things, Mr. Douglas. How long were you there, Ms. Pettybone?"

"About twenty minutes, maybe more."

"Can you tell me what you and Mr. Dorsey did talk about?"

"As I said, I answered questions about the company and our processes."

"Twenty minutes to talk about company processes and such, huh?" Pryor stood up, and so did his silent partner, Wiggins. "Well, I guess if a pretty lady like yourself was settin' in my office, I'd wanna talk about processes for as long as I could too. Thank you, folks, for your time. I'll be in touch if we have any more questions."

Marcus handed Pryor his card. "We're always available to answer any questions at any time."

Once the detectives were gone, Angela returned to Marcus in the living room.

"You wanna tell me now what's going on?"

"I was gonna tell you about that," Angela said, unable to look Marcus in the eye.

"I don't know if you realize it, but I could tell by the questions and his attitude that they consider you a suspect in this guy's murder."

"You really think so?"

"You need to tell me everything, Angela."

Angela sat down on the couch and took a deep breath. "What I told the police is pretty much the way it went."

"Pretty much, Angela?"

"Pretty much."

"What's different?"

"Robert was there."

Marcus let his head fall into the palms of his hands. "You need to tell me everything, Angela. I can't help you if you don't tell me the truth."

"Okay, Marcus," Angela said, and gave him the look that used to make Marcus weak. "You really think they consider me a suspect?"

Marcus laughed a little. "Yes, Angela, I think they do. Pryor wanted to know about the nature of your relationship with Dorsey. He was trying to sniff out a motive. And the way he pressed you about the argument and what you were supposed to have said, he's got a witness that heard you say it. Yeah, you're a suspect, all right. The only reason you're not in custody right now is that I was here."

"He didn't anticipate me having my lawyer present."

"Now he'll have to make sure all his ducks are

in a row before he comes back at you. But he'll be back, you can take that to the bank."

"Okay. I don't know what exactly Floyd and Robert were involved in together. At first, Robert said if the deal went through that he would be set for a while. But something happened to change that."

"What?"

"I don't know."

"I'm gonna assume that he told you to go to that meeting."

"That's right."

"Why?"

"He didn't like the way things were going, and he wanted to catch Floyd off guard. See if he could find out what Floyd was up to. So he sent me in alone and he went around to Floyd's private entrance and waited for me to call him."

"If it was Floyd's private entrance, how did Robert get in?"

"I'm not sure. Maybe Floyd gave him a key."

"What were you supposed to say to get him talking?"

"I was supposed to act like I knew what they were doing and tell him that Robert had been acting very strange lately, and that I thought he wanted to back out of the deal. That's when Floyd lost it and started yelling at me."

"So there was an argument?"

"Yes. When he started yelling Robert came in. They started arguing with each other. Then Robert said that Floyd was crazy and that what he was doing was gonna get him killed. That's when I said, 'Stop it.'"

"What happened after that?"

"Robert stormed out of there. I said a few words to Floyd to try to calm things down. When I saw that wasn't doing any good, I got out of there too. But Floyd was alive when I left him."

Chapter 7

Marcus walked out of Angela's house and headed for his car. He had stayed longer than he had expected, because he wasn't expecting more cops to show up about another murder. In light of that murder, Marcus had a lot more questions to ask, but he had appointments that he had to keep that afternoon in his office. While he drove downtown, Marcus called Garrett.

"I was just about to call you," Garrett said as soon as he answered the phone.

"What you got?"

"Not much. Information is coming out slowly. Other than the fact that the FBI is involved in the investigation, there's not much."

"FBI?"

"You heard me. The fuckin' FBI."

"Why would the FBI be involved in this, unless it's connected to something federal? I know somebody that might be able to tell us something."

"Who's that?"

"Special Agent Lawrence Rietman."

"I remember him. He was the agent in charge of the Hudson/Ferguson investigation."

"Maybe he can shine a light on this thing for us. But in the meantime, we should go at this from another angle. See what you can find out about Integrated."

"I'm way ahead of you. That's where I'm going now."

"With everybody being so tight-lipped, how are you planning on getting in?"

"You leave that to me."

"This is big, so whatever you do, be careful."

"You know what a careful guy I am, Marcus," Garrett said, and felt for his gun.

"You got any other good news for me?" Marcus asked, wanting to know if he had a chance to check on Panthea Daniels.

"I was able to find out that Stephanie Covey's apartment was ransacked. Killer was looking for something."

"Any idea what they were looking for?"

"Not that anybody's talking about."

"Anything else?"

"Nothing concrete. Everything is just rumors. The body was bound and gagged and there's some talk about Stephanie Covey being tortured before she was killed. But like I said, that's all just speculation at this point."

"That may explain why they're not all that hot on Angela even though she was spotted leaving the scene. Robert Covey looks better for this. He still hasn't surfaced yet. See if you can find him. And I got something else for you to look into."

"Damn, Marcus, first you drop this juicy shit on me and now you got more work. This might turn out to be a good month after all."

"You know, Garrett, if things are that tight for you, I could—"

"Offer me some charity. Thanks, but no, thanks. You just keep me working, that's all I need is to work."

"What I was going to say is, if you want me to, we could go back to the judge to see if we can't get you some relief. I know this is a load for you to carry."

"Sorry. Maybe I'm just a little sensitive about that right now. But hold up on going back to the judge for right now. Something is going on with Paven and the kids."

"Everything all right?"

"I'm not sure, but we'll talk about it the next time I see you."

"You know, Garrett, anything you need, I'm there for you. You know that, right?"

"Yeah, I know that, and I appreciate it, I really do. But you keep me workin' and I'll be cool. Now what else you got for me?"

"I need you to get with a Gwinnett County detective named Pryor and look into the murder of a Floyd Dorsey."

"Who's the client?"

"Same client. While I was at her house, Pryor came to question her about the murder."

"She more of a suspect in this one?"

"That was the impression I got. I think my being there threw him, so he didn't push her as hard as he might have wanted."

"I'm almost at Integrated now. When I get finished here, I'll go run down Detective Pryor. See what he got for me. But I'll tell you something about your girl, big dawg. There's a whole lot more to this than she's telling you."

"Really, you think?" Marcus laughed. "These days, I think every woman's got something she's not telling."

"Oh yeah. I haven't had a chance to check on Panthea Daniels, but I'm gonna get to that too."

As much as Marcus hated to say it, "That's back burner. Stay on this."

"I'll call you back when I have something," Garrett told Marcus, and ended the call.

Garrett pulled into the parking lot at Integrated Data Systems and got out of his car. Marcus was right about one thing: with everybody keeping information so close to the vest, Garrett was sure that nobody would want to talk to a *private* investigator. But if he were a cop, that would improve the odds considerably.

With that thought in mind, Garrett opened up his trunk and took out his briefcase. "Now, where is that damn thing?" After digging around in the briefcase, he found what he was looking for. His old Atlanta police detective's badge.

Under normal circumstances, Garrett would have gone right to the top. The top at Integrated was Brandon Marley; he'd been ill and at a time like this he would most likely be mourning the death of his daughter.

Garrett found that Anthony Marley was now running the company in his older brother's place. He flashed his old badge and bluffed his way into a seat in Anthony Marley's reception area. After he'd waited for almost an hour, all the while fearing that a real cop would show up and blow his cover, the receptionist finally looked in his direction.

"Mr. Marley will see you now."

"Thank you," Garrett said, and sprang to his feet.

The receptionist showed Garrett into the office and he was immediately overwhelmed by the sheer size of it. The room was big. And so was everything else in it. Big, plush couch, big chairs, big pictures on the walls, and a big desk in the center of the room. Then his eyes focused on the little man standing behind the desk.

"Come in, Detective. Have a seat," Anthony Marley said. He was a frail-looking man who stood five feet six inches tall and was much younger than his brother, who was well into his sixties.

"Thank you, Mr. Marley. I want to offer my condolences for your niece."

"Thank you, Detective. She was a special person. The family is devastated by this."

"I can only imagine how you must feel. Again, you have my deepest sympathy. I won't take up a lot of your time. I know you're a busy man and I appreciate you taking the time to talk to me."

"No trouble at all. Whatever I can do to help. In

fact, I was wondering when somebody was gonna get around to talking to me."

"No one from the department has been here?" Garrett asked in surprise.

"Oh no. We had police and FBI agents in and out of here for the last two days. I was just pointing out that you're the first one to talk to me, Detective— I didn't catch the name."

"Brunet, John Brunet."

"Well, Detective Brunet, what can I tell you?"

"Well, that's what I'm here to find out, what you can tell me."

"I'm not sure I understand."

"Unless I've been misinformed, you don't have any information about the murder, so anything you can tell me would be helpful."

"Oh," Marley said, and looked away.

Garrett could tell that he already felt left out of what was going on. He hoped that the need to be included would make Marley tell him anything he felt he knew, or at the very least, he might be able to confirm some of the rumors.

"I can tell you one thing," Marley said quickly.

"What's that, Mr. Marley?"

"That you need to be looking for her husband, Robert Covey."

"What makes you say that, sir?"

"He's a shameless opportunist. Robert was a low-level programmer that saw my niece, Stephanie, as an opportunity. The only reason he married her was for what she could do for him."

"As tasteless as that is, it doesn't make him a

killer. So, is there anything about the crime itself that leads you to believe that Robert Covey murdered your niece?"

"I don't know."

"Think, Mr. Marley, you work with this man. Is this something that he's capable of?"

"I think so."

"Then think, Mr. Marley. Tell me why you believe that he killed your niece. There's a piece that I need, something that puts him in that apartment with a reason to kill her."

"I do know that Robert and Stephanie were having problems. I mean more problems than they usually have, and Stephanie finally moved out and filed for divorce. I do know the position that would put Robert in here at Integrated—and financially, once that divorce is final."

"What position is that? I can pretty much figure what will happen to him here. I'm more interested in the financial aspect you mentioned."

"My brother married money, Detective. White money. I was only ten when Brandon married Amanda. Too young to understand what that meant. But that's how he built this company, with her money and the connections that kind of money brings. Anyway, when Amanda died, she left most of her estate to Stephanie. My niece is a wealthy woman. Not rich, but wealthy."

"That gives him a motive. Now think, Mr. Marley, think about the crime and his motive, and give me something that puts him in that apartment. Now think. Your niece is tied up and gagged."

"Yes."

"He tortured her."

"Yes."

"Searched the place."

"Yes."

"And when he didn't find what he was looking for, or found it, then he killed her. Robert killed her. What was he looking for, Mr. Marley? Fill in the blanks for me, so I can put this animal away for a long time."

"I wish I could, Detective," Marley said, shaking his head. "But I just can't think of anything."

"I understand, Mr. Marley. You've already been most helpful." And he had been. Garrett now knew that Stephanie Covey was, in fact, bound and gagged, tortured, and then murdered and he had even given Garrett a motive for the crime. "I only have a couple more questions to ask. You said earlier that Robert and Stephanie were having more problems than they usually did. What did you mean by that?"

"Robert is a dog—a low-life dog. He's cheated on Stephanie from the day they got involved. The latest one is that assistant of his. I don't know how or why Stephanie tolerated his shit for as long as she had."

"Did Stephanie ever catch him, or can you say for sure that he was cheating on her?"

"Of course she caught him, many times. He flaunted them in her face all the time."

"Do you know if she knew about him and his assistant?"

"Now, I can't say for sure if Stephanie knew about Angela or not."

"What is her name?"

"Angela Pettybone, an absolutely irresistible woman, who is that rare combination of beauty and intellect. Robert simply had to have her."

Garrett looked and listened to the way Marley talked about Angela, and he could tell one thing. "You want her too, don't you, Mr. Marley? Just an observation, sir. You don't have to answer."

"But the answer is yes. You'll understand why if you ever meet her."

"Is she in? I can go by there right now." Garrett laughed and so did Marley.

"No, I'm afraid she's not in today. But that may be the missing piece you've been looking for, Detective."

"Angela Pettybone, you mean?"

"Yes. Maybe his need to have her led him to kill his wife."

"It wouldn't be the first time. One last question. Is there anyone that is in the office today that was close to Robert? Somebody he might have confided in?"

"That would be Chuck Prentice. Chuck and Robert worked very closely together for years. But unfortunately he was murdered two weeks ago."

"What can you tell me about that?"

"Not much. His body was found in his car. Shot to death."

"That's unfortunate. Is there anybody else?"

"I believe Chuck was friends with Dennis Cline."

"And where can I find him?"

"R-and-D department."

Garrett stood up and extended his hand to Marley. "Thank you, Mr. Marley. You have been a big help to me."

When he left Marley's office and found out how to get to the R&D department, Garrett made his way there and hoped that no other law enforcement officers were in the area. On the way there, he thought about how much information he got from Marley. *Money—motive for murder since the world began*, Garrett thought.

When Garrett got to the R&D department he was escorted to Cline's small office.

"Dennis Cline?"

"Yes."

"I'm Detective Brunet," Garrett said, and flashed his old badge again. "Would you mind if I ask you a couple of questions about Chuck Prentice?"

"You're investigating Chuck's murder?"

"No, I'm investigating the murder of Stephanie Covey. I understand from Mr. Marley that Chuck and Robert were friends. I wanted to ask you if there was anything that you can tell me that might be helpful."

"Would you mind shutting that door, Detective?"

Garrett got up and closed the door and returned to his seat. "Like I told the other detective, Chuck told me that Robert was cheating on Stephanie with somebody here in the office, and that bothered him."

"Why would it bother him?"

"He said it was because as much as Robert cheated on Stephanie, he lost his mind when he heard that Chuck was having an affair with Stephanie."

"Was he?"

"Was he what?"

"Was Chuck having an affair with Stephanie?"

"I don't know for sure. All I know is that a couple of days before Chuck was murdered, he and Robert were having a very heated argument in Robert's office. When I asked him what they were arguing about, that's what he told me. But he never said whether he was having an affair with Stephanie."

When Garrett left Integrated Data Systems, he left with exactly what he came for, and much more than he had expected. The pieces to Stephanie Covey's murder were falling into place. Robert Covey murdered his wife. And might have killed Chuck Prentice too.

Garrett knew that if he called Marcus now, he would tell him to check with the Atlanta police and look into Chuck Prentice's murder. That would be his next stop after he talked to the Gwinnett County Police about Floyd Dorsey. But there was something more important that he had to do first.

Chapter 8

It wasn't quite two o'clock in the afternoon when Garrett turned down Woodhurst Way and parked in front of the house that he used to live in, and still paid for.

Even though everything that Marcus had him working on was important, to Garrett, this was much more important. Garrett walked up to the front door like he was on a mission, which he was. If what Aleana told him was true, and he had no reason to believe it wasn't, things had gotten totally out of control with his family. And for whatever reason, Paven had made his children promise not to tell him what was going on. This was unacceptable to him.

Garrett was about to let himself in and go straight to his son Gary's room, but he rang the bell and waited to see if anybody would answer. If Paven was there, she did deserve her privacy.

When no one answered the door, Garrett let himself in and went straight to Gary's room, but not really expecting to find him. After a quick turn around the house to make sure that neither Gary nor Paven was there, Garrett got back in his car and drove around the maze of streets that made up the Hidden Hills subdivision.

He found Gary standing in somebody's driveway, listening to loud music with four other boys that looked like they were older than him. Garrett got out of his car and started walking toward the house.

"Ain't that your pops, G?" one of the boys asked.

"Oh, shit," Gary said, and quickly started walking toward him. "Hey, Daddy," he said, but Garrett walked past him and right up to the other four boys.

"How you young men doing today?" Garrett said, and looked each one over. "I know you. Reggie, ain't it?"

"Yes, sir. How you doin', Mr. Mason?"

"I'm not even gonna ask why you ain't in school. I'm just gonna assume that you got caught smokin' weed with that jackass there and we'll leave it at that."

"Yes, sir."

Garrett looked at his son and then back at the boys. "I don't know you three. I just wanted to see who my son was hangin' around with. You young men have a good day."

Garrett turned, walked away, and stopped in front of his son. He stood there for a second or two, but Gary wouldn't make eye contact with him. "I'm not gonna say nothing about your pants falling off your ass. Come on, ride with me," Garrett said, and walked to his car with Gary on his heels.

They drove for a while without speaking; Gary looking out the window with his arms folded across his chest. Finally, Gary broke the silence. "Where we goin'?"

"Police station."

"For what!"

"Calm down, Gary. You just stupid, you ain't a criminal yet, are you?"

"No!"

"So, as far as I know being stupid ain't a crime."

"So, what we goin' there for?"

"I'm workin'."

"Naturally. That's all you ever do," Gary said, and folded his arms across his chest.

"Look, I'm sorry if I embarrassed you—"

"Why I gotta be a jackass?"

"'Cause you are. It's bad enough that you're smokin' weed. Why you gotta do it in the bathroom where you know you're gonna get caught?"

"How was I supposed to know that we'd get caught?"

"'Cause weed smells, jackass. People can smell it, and that's how you got caught."

"Nah, that ain't what happened. Somebody snitched on us."

"Oh, so it's their fault that you got caught?"

"Yeah. If they wasn't so busy snitchin', we wouldn'ta got caught."

"Or maybe you shoulda got a lookout to tell you that somebody was coming, jackass. How could you be so stupid, Gary?"

Gary folded his arms again and looked out the window. Garrett looked over at him while he drove.

"How you find out?"

"Wanna know who snitched on you so you can blame them?" Gary said nothing. "You are fifteen years old. You have got to start taking responsibility for what you do. You got caught smokin' weed. You're the one that got suspended for what you did. You got suspended. You got me talkin' to you about it. You're responsible for this, Gary. Nobody but you. Look, you can go through life blaming other people for what you do, but in the end, it all comes back to you."

"I know that."

"You gotta start thinking about what you do and the consequences of what you do before you do it. Start taking responsibility so you can be—"

"More like you?"

And what would be so bad about that? Garrett asked himself instead of asking Gary. They needed to talk, not argue. Garrett took a deep breath. "I'm not saying that you gotta be like me, just make something of yourself."

Gary looked over at his father while he drove. "Can I ask you something?"

"What?" Garrett asked, still feeling the bite of Gary's last comment.

"You work hard every day, Daddy. You been workin' hard every day since I can remember. You worked hard and made something of yourself. What did it get you?"

"What?"

"What did all that work get you? All you got to show for all your hard work is that rinky-dink apartment."

"I—"

"Dad, Mom is cold taking advantage of you."

"So I been hearing."

"I knew it was Aleana that snitched me out. But I bet she didn't tell you what she was doin', did she?"

"What she doin'?"

"Nah, Dad, I ain't goin' out like that. I can't be mad at her for snitchin', and then I turn and snitch on her. That's not how I roll."

"How do you roll?"

"I ain't no snitch and I ain't gonna let no—nobody take advantage of me."

"You gotta get yours, right?"

"That's right, I gotta get mine," Gary said as they pulled into the parking lot at the Gwinnett County Sheriff's Office on University Parkway.

"If I had that attitude—'I gotta get mine'—you'd be on the street with your no-workin' mama and I'd be living in the house I'm payin' for." Garrett took out his gun, then reached over and opened the glove compartment.

"Can I see it?"

"You are a jackass for even asking me that question." Garrett put the gun in the glove compartment and locked it. "Wait here. This won't take long. And don't even think about pickin' the lock."

"You shouldn't have taught me how."

Garrett slammed the door and walked toward the building. Maybe he shouldn't have taught Gary how to pick a lock, but he had tried to teach him right from wrong and things like honor and loyalty. This was an important time in Gary's life. He was becoming a man, probably thought he was. From what Garrett could see, Gary, suspended from school for fighting and smoking weed, was on the wrong path. Garrett needed to be more involved in his life.

It wasn't long after that Garrett was shaking hands with Detective Pryor. "My name is Garrett Mason. I'm a private investigator, working for Marcus Douglas. You spoke with him earlier today with his client Angela Pettybone."

"Yes, Ms. Pettybone," Pryor said. "Why don't we talk in my office?" Pryor turned quickly and walked away. "So, Mason, is it? What's your background?"

"I used to work for the Atlanta police. But that's been some years," Garrett said as they walked.

"Reason I ask is 'cause you look familiar, like we worked together before. I never forget a face. Names I ain't shit with, but faces, I got 'em."

"I used to be with the Red-Dog Unit." The Atlanta police Red-Dog Unit provided an aggressive presence in areas that had a high incidence of street drug sales and drug-related crimes. Since his corruption case stemmed from his activities while he was a member of that unit, it was a subject that Garrett was a little sensitive about.

"That must be it," Pryor said as they arrived at his office. "Why don't you come on in and have a seat?"

"Thank you," Garrett said, and sat down.

"So. What's it like being a private investigator?"

"It pays the bills. Every once in a while you get

a little action, but most of the time it's following people, taking pictures, and askin' a whole bunch of questions."

Pryor laughed. "'Bout like this here."

"Just like this here."

"Enough of this small talk. What can I do for you?"

"I was hoping you would give me some information about Floyd Dorsey."

"That matter is still under investigation. Ms. Pettybone hasn't been charged in the matter. If and when she is charged, I'm sure the DA's office will provide Mr. Douglas with all that information from our investigation."

"I understand that. But I like to get out in front of things, you know. Know where I'm goin' before I go there."

"That's the cop in you. Likes to proceed on sure ground. I can understand that." Pryor sat back in his chair and allowed it to swivel a bit while he looked at Garrett. "Tell you what I'm gonna do. I'm gonna give you part of what you came here for. I'm gonna tell about the crime, but not how it relates to Ms. Pettybone. Is that fair?"

"More than fair."

"Besides, if you was any kind of cop, you'd find out anyway. Just take you a while."

Garrett laughed a little. "That's true."

"The coroner has established that Mr. Dorsey was murdered at approximately seven forty-five p.m., with a Tcc P 11. He was shot once in the head at close range. No sign of forced entry, and nothing in the office was disturbed. That's 'bout all I care to share right now."

Garrett stood up, taking that as a clear indication that it was time for him to go. "I appreciate that. Thanks for talking to me."

"I'll tell you one other thing, and this is more of a personal observation than anything else."

"What's that, Detective?"

"Ms. Pettybone is a fine-looking woman, very professional, very businesslike. She's the kind of woman that can answer all your questions without giving you any information. That bothers me."

"I've never met her."

"If you did, you'd know what I mean."

"I'm sure we'll talk again," Garrett said, and walked out of the office.

"You can count on that," Pryor said loud enough for Garrett to hear him. He left the building thinking not only about the crime, but also about Angela Pettybone. Pryor's description of her wasn't flattering. In fact, he all but called her a liar. At best, he didn't believe Angela's story.

When he reached his car, Garrett got in and turned down the radio. "That didn't take long," he said, and opened the glove compartment to be sure his gun was still there.

"Nope," Gary replied, and sat up straight in the seat. "Where we goin' now?"

"Why? Where you gotta be?"

"Nowhere."

"Then ride with me."

"I don't have a choice, do I?"

"Not really," Garrett said, and took out his cell.

"You can still tell me where we goin'."

"Be quiet. I'm on the phone. Hey, Janise, it's Garrett. Is he in?"

"He is," Janise replied.

"Tell him I'm on my way, and that I got something for him." Garrett ended the call. "We're going to see Mr. Douglas," he told Gary.

"Cool. Mr. Douglas is the man," Gary said enthusiastically, sitting up in his seat.

"So, Mr. Douglas is the man, huh?"

"Yup."

"Why is that?"

"Come on, Dad. Mr. Douglas is rollin' a seven series BMW, he got that big house, wearin' them nice suits all the time. And, Dad, Mr. D always got the fly women. Mr. Douglas is paid. I'ma be paid like that."

"Not if you keep smokin' weed in school!" Garrett yelled. He drove the rest of the way to Marcus's office without saying anything else. He did put a call in to John Brunet to get information about the murder of Chuck Prentice. Brunet promised to look into it and get back to Garrett, but after that, not a word. He didn't even say anything when Gary turned up the radio. Every once in a while he glanced over at his son. He felt devalued in his son's eyes. Like what he did had no value except to be taken advantage of by his mother. *All you got to show for all your hard work is that rinky-dink apartment.*

When Garrett arrived at Marcus's office and went in, he told Gary to wait in the lobby while he took care of his business. He looked back at Gary before going in; Garrett felt like a failure in his son's eyes. He had always tried to instill in his son the value of hard work—his values. The values he lived his life by. Now it seemed that Gary assessed those values and deemed them to have none.

Garrett closed the door to the office and tried to do the same with his family issues. "I just got one question to ask you, Marcus."

"What's that, Garrett?"

"Where do you find these women?"

Marcus laughed. "They usually find me. They walk through that door, sit in that chair, and—"

"Lie like hell, do some killin' maybe. Or at best, not tell you everything."

"What now?"

"Next time you talk to your client, why don't you ask her if she thinks talking to Chuck Prentice is a good idea?"

"Why, what's up with Chuck?"

"Chuck's dead."

"Chuck's dead?"

"That's what I said."

"Okay, now who's Chuck?"

"Chuck *was* a lead programmer at Integrated. He was also a very good friend of Robert Covey. He was murdered two weeks ago."

"You're going to tell me how that relates to Angela."

"The way I get it is that Chuck was having an affair with Stephanie Covey. Robert found out about it, they argued about it at work in front of witnesses."

"Robert kills Chuck, he confronts Stephanie and kills her too. Both killed in a jealous rage."

"Chuck I go along with, but there's more to him killing Stephanie than just jealousy," Garrett said.

"What makes you say that?"

"I have reasonable confirmation that Stephanie Covey was bound, gagged, tortured, and the apartment was searched before she was killed, or she was killed and then the apartment was searched."

"Impossible to tell which."

"But if it is the husband, what's he looking for? And if it's just about the affair, why torture her? Doesn't add up for me."

"What are the police saying about Chuck? Is Robert a suspect?"

"I put out some feelers, but I haven't got anything back yet. I went to see Detective Pryor about the other thing with Floyd Dorsey."

"What you get there?"

"Pryor said, and I quote, 'That matter's still under investigation. Ms. Pettybone ain't been charged in the matter. If and when she *is* charged, I'm sure the DA's office will provide Mr. Douglas with all the information from his investigation,' or words to that effect."

"Nice."

"But he did tell me that the coroner established that Dorsey was shot once in the head at close range, with a Tec P-11, about seven forty-five p.m. There was no sign of forced entry and nothing in the office was disturbed. And that's 'bout all he cared to share."

"Well, that was nice of him."

"He's got something on her."

"I know you're gonna tell me why you say that."

"I am." Garrett leaned forward. "He was willing to share what he called a personal observation."

"What's that?"

"He said, and again, I'm trying to quote him. He said, 'Ms. Pettybone is a fine woman, very professional, businesslike.'"

"I'll go along with that. She is something."

"But then he said she's the kind of woman that can answer all your questions without giving you any information. And that bothers him."

"That bothers me that he would say that. I agree he has something on her. But I can see why he would think that. He's probably used to handling people. But Angela handled him, pissed him off a couple of times with her answers. She even used me to do it once."

"How's that?"

"Angela told him about a project that Integrated and Dorsey's company were joint-venturing on, and Pryor asked her what the project was about. Angela looked over at me and gave me this look like, *get him off me, Marcus*." Both men laughed. "And I fell right in line, and gave him some crap about due to the sensitive nature of the project, I'd have to ask my client not to answer that question at this time."

"She may not be a strong suspect in Stephanie Covey's murder, only because the husband looks better for it. But if I had to offer an opinion, I'd say

Pryor thinks she killed Dorsey. He just hasn't got all the pieces yet."

"Tec P-11 is a small gun, isn't it?" Marcus asked.

"Just the right size for a professional business-woman's handbag."

"Anything else?"

"Stephanie Covey's uncle, Anthony Marley, thinks Robert had a financial motive to kill her. And he'll tell the police that as soon as one asks him."

"He hasn't talked to the police?"

"No."

"How'd you talk to him?"

"As far as you know, I didn't. And I didn't talk to Dennis Cline about Chuck and Stephanie Covey having an affair either."

"I don't get it."

"You don't need to. Just remember that it wasn't me."

Chapter 9

Marcus sat back in his chair and tried to digest all the information and opinions that Garrett had just presented him with. He thought about what Pryor said about Angela's ability to answer questions without giving any information, and wondered how much of that he had fallen prey to. How much had he allowed his objectivity to be compromised by their past friendship, and clouded further by his infatuation with her and her beauty?

If he was going to remain her lawyer, Marcus was going to have to separate himself from those feelings and focus on preparing to defend her in a series of murders that might or might not be connected to the others, but all were connected to her and Robert Covey.

"You start looking into what kind of business Covey and Dorsey were into, and I'll attack it from my angle," Marcus told Garrett.

"It does seem to be the one thing that nobody is

willing to talk about. But I got the kids this weekend. Gary's out in the lobby waiting for me."

"Is he really? Damn, I haven't seen Gary in a
couple of years."

"Well, come on and say hello. I know he'd love
to see you," Garrett said as he and Marcus got up
and went into the lobby.

When Gary saw them coming, he sprang to his
feet and a big smile washed over his face. He even
pulled up his pants. "How you doin', Mr. Douglas?"

"I'm great, Gary. But look at you. Is that a mus-
tache I see trying to grow?" Marcus said, and
poked at Gary's upper lip.

"Yeah, I'm tryin' ta do a little somethin', you
know. You looking sharp, as always."

Marcus brushed his shoulders off. "Yeah, well,
you know, I'm tryin' ta do a little somethin'." He
kidded with Gary.

Garrett stood back with his arms folded across
his chest and looked on as Marcus and Gary continued, until he couldn't stand it anymore. "Gary
says he gonna be paid like you one day."

"That's great, Gary. If you set a goal and work
hard to make it happen, I know you can do it,"
Marcus said, and patted Gary on the shoulder for
encouragement. Gary glared at his father.

"That's not gonna happen," Garrett said.

"Why is that?" Marcus asked.

"Because Gary doesn't see the value in working
hard."

"Really? Why is that, Gary?"

"'Cause he looks at all the hard work I did for

all these years, and says that I have nothing to show for it but my rinky-dink apartment," Garrett said before Gary could answer.

"It is kind of small, Garrett. You could do better than that," Marcus said, and Gary gave him five.

"See, Dad, Mr. Douglas agrees with me. Tell him, Mr. Douglas, Mom is cold taking advantage of him. But I'm just a kid, he won't listen to me."

"First, let's get something straight. I agree that your mom is cold taking advantage of him, but not with what you think about hard work. You have to work hard for everything you get in this world."

"You tell him, Marcus. I'm just his father. He won't listen to me. He thinks you got it goin' on 'cause you rollin' a BMW and you got all the fly women. He already told you how he feels about the way you dress."

"Gary, I worked very hard for years to get where I am. And you know what? I still work hard every day, just like your father does. The only difference between your father and me is that he had to leave school early to support you guys. And in case you didn't know, your father is a very successful private investigator. He's just on a run of tough financial times. Things that I really wish he'd let me do something about. But your father is a very proud man."

"Okay, okay, men. Okay." Garrett put up his hands. "I surrender. Go on and do what you gotta do, Marcus." Garrett had decided that Gary was gonna live with him for a while. He would see what was going on with Paven, and if she wasn't gonna do the right thing for her children, he would try to get custody of the girls too.

Garrett would have a little talk with Monique about her mouth, and later that night when he saw her, he would find out what it was that Aleana was into that her brother wouldn't talk about. But right now Gary needed his father. "Let's go, Gary, we've taken up enough of Mr. Douglas's time. I'll get on that Covey and Dorsey business first thing Monday morning. And I'll call you when I get something on Chuck Prentice," Garrett said as he and Gary walked away.

"Thanks for not tellin' him about the weed thing, Dad," Gary said as they got on the elevator.

After the Mason men left the building, Marcus went back to his office but he didn't stay there for long. He braved rush-hour traffic, driving into the sunset on I-20, on his way to Angela's house. While he drove, Marcus had to ask himself if he was going to talk about the situation, or was her situation just a convenient excuse to be with Angela? The answer was simple. What he had learned about her situation, though important, could have waited until Monday.

Since the time Marcus left her house to go back to his office, Angela had been sitting on her deck thinking about her situation. During that time she had tried to call Robert at least four times. Not wanting to believe that he killed Stephanie, Angela couldn't understand why he had just disappeared like this. No matter what he had done, she felt she deserved better than this. She thought she meant more to him.

And what had he gotten her involved in? If Marcus was right, she would be in jail for killing Floyd. Robert said he didn't kill him and at the time she believed him. But she was his alibi, she told the police that she went to that meeting by herself in his place.

When the doorbell rang, it caught Angela off guard. Her first thought was that maybe it was Robert, and she hurried to the door. She was genuinely surprised when she opened the door and saw Marcus standing there.

"I hope you don't mind me stopping by like this, Angela. But I've gotten some information based on what you told me and I think we need to discuss it."

"Sure, Marcus," Angela said, and stepped aside, disappointed that it wasn't Robert. She needed him to tell her what was going on. "Come in, please."

"Thank you."

"I was just about to fix myself a drink. Can I get you something?"

"Hennessey, if you have it. Otherwise, anything is fine." Marcus followed Angela to the bar in her living room.

"I believe I have some Hennessey." Angela moved a few bottles in her liquor cabinet. "Yes, I do. How do you take it?"

"Straight is fine."

"So, tell me this information that got you to drive all the way out here. Was traffic bad?"

"Yes, it was, and how do you stand it driving into the sun like that?"

"You get used to it, I guess." Angela poured Marcus a glass of Hennessey, and then began to fix her own.

"I had my investigator ask a few questions, and there is a lot more going on here."

"Like what?"

"Like what is the FBI doing involved in Stephanie Covey's murder?" Marcus asked to see how she'd react.

"I don't know," Angela said without showing any reaction to the news. Marcus would have assumed that the FBI's involvement in a case that she had been questioned about would elicit some response from her. But Angela simply finished fixing her drink, sat down next to Marcus, and waited for him to continue. "Was there anything else?"

"No, Angela, there really is nothing else." Marcus was frustrated by her casual attitude. "Just that you're a suspect in two murders. If the police charged Robert with his wife's murder, you could be implicated as a conspirator or named as an accomplice because of the nature of your relationship with him. From the looks of it, you're going to be charged in Floyd Dorsey's murder. You need to tell Pryor the truth."

"What truth is that?" Angela asked casually.

"That Robert was actually there that day with you and Dorsey. That it was the two of them arguing, and that's why you said, 'Stop this.'"

"I understand that, Marcus."

"Angela, I honestly don't think you do. Do you know where Robert is?"

"I already told you that I don't know where he is."

"Do you understand that if they can't find him, they will settle for you?"

"I understand!" Angela shouted.

"Why did you lie to the police about Robert being there? Why are you protecting him?"

"Isn't it obvious to you, Marcus?"

Marcus looked at Angela. "You're in love with him."

"Yes. I love him, and right or wrong, I still love him and I'll do whatever I have to do to protect him."

"Does that include going to jail for him?"

"Let's hope it doesn't get to that." Angela got up and went to fix herself another drink. She had allowed Marcus to rattle her, to back her into a corner. It was a position she wasn't used to, but she knew how to come out of it. "I didn't kill anybody," she said forcefully. "And I wasn't part of any conspiracy to kill anybody."

"Then why won't you tell me the truth? I can't help you if you don't tell me the truth."

"I didn't ask for your—" Angela paused and the expression on her face softened into a smile. "I was about to say that I didn't ask for your help, but that wouldn't be quite true, would it?"

"No, Angela, it wouldn't. You did call me and ask me to come out here. I thought it was because you wanted me to help you."

"Maybe I overreacted when I called you."

Marcus finished his drink and stood up. "Then I guess it's time for me to go."

"No, Marcus. Don't go. I understand the position I'm in and I know that I need your help."

"Then you have got to start telling me the truth, Angela."

Angela picked up Marcus's glass and began to pour him another drink. "I'll make you a deal."

"What's that?"

"You sit down and have another drink with me, and I'll tell you whatever you want to know. Is that a win-win, or what?" Angela posted her best power smile.

Marcus smiled and sat back down. "Where is Robert?"

"I really don't know where Robert is. You have got to believe that."

"Okay. Where might he be?"

"I don't know."

"Come on, Angela. You're his personal assistant and his lover, you have got to have some idea where he might be."

"I've checked all the places I thought he might be. And I really don't appreciate the condescending way you said *his lover*."

"I'm sorry. I didn't mean anything by it."

"I guess you never fell in love with somebody else's woman, Marcus? I guess you don't know what it's like to know that everything about what you're feeling is wrong, but you still feel it anyway. You can't really understand what it feels like to deny those feelings because you know that it is wrong, on so many levels, but you feel empty, like nothing in the world matters except being with them. Have you ever tried to stop loving somebody, but knowing that you never will?"

"I understand, Angela. I understand better than you know." It was exactly how he felt the love he had for her was at one time. And it was only the passage of time that allowed him to escape those feelings. "But it doesn't change the fact that you're in this situation and regardless of how you feel about Robert, you have got to think about yourself. I believe that you're not involved in this mess, whatever it is, but right now you're tailor-made to step off for it."

"Okay, Marcus. I said I would tell you what I know, but I don't know much. I don't know what Robert and Floyd were involved in, I just know that Robert said if the deal went through he would be set."

"Let's start there. My sources tell me that Robert had some financial inducement to kill his wife. What can you tell me about that?"

"Robert and I planned to be together. He wanted to divorce Stephanie and for us to get married, but if he did that he would lose everything. Divorcing her meant that he would definitely lose his position, if not his career. Robert said this deal would put us in a position that we needed to be in. We planned to start our own company."

"You understand, of course, that what you just told me puts you in the seat next to him at his murder trial?"

Angela paused and thought about what Marcus meant. "I think I do, but explain it to me anyway."

"Let me tell you what the police will hear from the statement you just made. You said that you and Robert planned to be together, but he would lose everything if he divorced her. The operative word is 'planned.' You said Robert's deal with Floyd Dorsey would set him up and the two of you planned to start your own business. Now, whether that's how it happened or not, Stephanie Covey finds out about the relationship between you and Robert and she leaves him. You stated that Robert knew that if she divorced him he would lose his job and her money, so now the two of you, because of the plan you spoke of, have a strong motive for murdering her.

"Now let's talk about Floyd Dorsey. Robert has a deal going with Dorsey. As you stated, that deal would allow the two of you to get out from under Stephanie, get married, and start your own business. But something went wrong and Robert and Floyd argued over it, and that same night Floyd Dorsey turned up dead. Witnesses place you at the scene."

Marcus took a sip of his drink and looked at Angela. He could tell from the look in her eyes and the expression on her face that Angela was starting to fully comprehend how this whole thing could turn around on her.

"Right now Pryor doesn't know about the importance of the deal for you and Robert, but there is still something that makes you look good to him. I think it stems from your relationship with Dorsey."

"There was no relationship."

"Then why does Pryor think so? Why was he pressing you so hard about that relationship if none existed?"

Angela dropped her head. "Floyd was in love with me," she said without looking up. "But there was never any interest on my part. But that didn't stop Floyd. He would call me every day, several times a day. It would always begin as a business conversation. He would ask me to clarify something for him, or to discuss some changes to their arrangement, but it would always turn personal."

"Did Dorsey know about you and Robert?"

"I don't think so. Robert and I went out of our way to keep it private."

"Tell me what happened that night."

"Before it was time to go to the meeting with Floyd, Robert got a call."

"From who?"

"I don't know. After he hung up, he said he wanted mc to go to see Floyd alone."

"Why?"

"Robert knew Floyd wanted me. He felt I could use that to find out what Floyd was doing."

"So you go to Floyd and act like you know what they were into and tell him that Robert's acting strange, and that he's wanting to back out of the deal. Floyd loses it and Robert comes in. What happened then?"

"They argued. Robert told Floyd that what he was doing was going to get them killed."

"What did Floyd say?"

"He said that won't happen. He said that he had

taken steps to protect them so that won't happen aga—so that won't happen."

"When the two of you left, Floyd was alive, right?"

"That's right, but after we left, Robert put me in a cab and he went back."

"Did you see or talk to him after that?"

"I saw him the next morning in the office. He said that Floyd still wouldn't listen to reason, so he was pulling out of the deal."

"When did you find out that Floyd was dead?"

"It was two days later, when the police came to question us."

"Who's us?"

"Me and Robert."

"So the police did talk to him, but he told the police that he wasn't there. That you went in his place. Looks like he set you up to take the fall for murder."

"Robert wouldn't do that. He loves me."

"Does Robert own a gun? A small gun?"

"Not that I know of. I've never heard Robert mention having a gun. But I know that Floyd had a small gun that he kept in his desk drawer. Why do you ask?"

"Floyd Dorsey was shot once at close range, with a Tec P-11. Because of its size, it's a very popular concealed weapon."

"You're saying that Floyd was shot with his own gun."

"That's exactly what I'm saying."

Chapter 10

It was late Friday night when Robert got to his condo on John Wesley Dobbs Avenue, not far from his office. After spending a fortune on hotels on nights that he was working late and didn't feel like driving out to Alpharetta, Angela had found it for him and got the lease in her name. It was only recently that it became their private hideaway.

She chose the loft, with its absolutely stunning view of downtown Atlanta. The hardwood floors throughout, granite, stainless steel appliances, floor-to-ceiling windows, and the large balcony off the great room had a little something to do with it too.

He never went to his house anymore; too many memories of Stephanie. Some good, some bad, but none that he felt like dealing with. Robert was in a good mood for a change; relaxed. Everything in his life was so chaotic. That's why when his friend Kiel called and invited him to Savannah to do some fishing for a couple of days, he jumped at the opportunity.

"You know, Kiel, that might be just what I need,"

Robert told him Wednesday afternoon when the idea of going out on Kiel's boat for a couple of days came up.

"Course it is. I've known you too long to steer you wrong. Besides, when was the last time you slacked off from work in the middle of the week?" Kiel asked.

"The last time I went fishing with you."

"Are you saying that I'm a bad influence?"

"No."

"You had a good time, right?"

"Right," Robert had to admit.

"Right. So I'm gonna pick you up in a few minutes and we're on our way."

"Sounds good. I'll leave my car here. We'll swing by the loft and pick up a few things and we'll hit the road."

"No can do. After I pick you up, my next stop is the pier. So I suggest that you do like your daddy taught you, and use the bathroom before you get in the car."

"Come on, Kiel, I gotta change clothes. I'm not going fishing in a suit."

"I got you some jeans, a T-shirt, and some size-fourteen sneakers, big foot."

"I need my stuff, you know, toothbrush, razor, deodorant?"

"Not that kind of trip. We're going to fish, get drunk, talk shit, and tell lies about how much pussy we're getting. You can bathe when you get back. Now stop making excuses."

"Okay. Let me call Angela and tell her that I'll be out of town for a couple of days."

"See, Robert, that's exactly what you're not going to do."

"I'm not?"

"No, you're not."

"You wanna tell me why?"

"You see, if you do that, sexy Angie will call you every ten minutes with some foolishness that either she could handle herself, or could have waited until you got back."

"You mean like she did the last time."

"It seemed like every time you got a fish on the hook, your phone rang, and what did you say?"

"What did I say?"

"You said, next time we go fishing, take my phone and lock it in the glove compartment and don't give it back to me until we get back. You do remember saying that, don't you?"

"Yes, I remember."

"Good. Now come outside and hand me your phone. I'm in the parking lot."

Now that Robert was feeling renewed, it was time to get back to work and put all this business with Floyd behind him. When he first came to Integrated, he was not the best programmer, but he was ambitious. So when he decided that he wanted to be a lead programmer, Robert understood that it was a political position, not one based on programming performance. A situation he corrected when he became director of R&D, but back then it was all office politics. With that understanding, Robert positioned himself to be considered for the R&D post. He shook all the right hands, made all the important interoffice alliances, had lunch with the right people, and went to all the company functions, which was something he never used to do.

That changed early one Monday morning, following one of those company functions. Robert was pouring a cup of coffee when Brandon Marley walked into the break room, coffee cup in hand. Naturally, he had seen Marley around the building, but he had never talked to him.

"Good morning, Robert."

"Good morning, Mr. Marley," Robert said, surprised that the big boss actually knew his name. He tried to pour faster.

"Did you enjoy yourself this weekend?"

"Yes, sir, but I didn't make it to the picnic."

"That's too bad. Everybody seemed to have a good time."

"To be honest with you, I really don't like going to those things."

"Really?" Marley asked as he poured his coffee. "Why not?"

"I'm kind of a private person, and—"

"You don't like people you work with knowing your business."

"Yes, sir, that's it exactly."

"I can understand that. I'm kind of the same way. Let me give you some advice, if I may."

"I'd be honored, sir," Robert said, and followed Marley out of the break room.

"An ambitious young man such as yourself

might want to consider going to those functions, because it gives people a chance to see you in a social setting. A different light, if you would. And more importantly, it gives you the same opportunity. Use that opportunity to observe your coworkers and study their behavior. You see, in that setting, they've let their guard down. Some of them will have had too much to drink."

"You see the real person then."

"Exactly. You see their weaknesses, and that may have some value in the future. Have a good day, Robert," Marley said as he disappeared into his office.

Robert had always been the type of person that was dedicated, determined, resolute, and persistent. One of his strengths was his ability to make decisions. That was a by-product of knowing what he wanted. Robert could see a situation, understand its value or significance, and how to make best use of it.

When the next company function came along, an after-work cocktail mixer to celebrate their first big government contract, Robert was there. That was the night that he first met Stephanie.

Almost from the day he began working at Integrated, Robert had heard that Marley had a daughter that lived in California, and how drop-dead gorgeous she was, and how unapproachable she was. Never having been one to buy into the hype, he took it as just that, hype. That was until she walked into the room that night. Being the kind of man he was, Robert knew right then that he had to have her. He walked right up to her and started a conversation. They talked for about fifteen minutes, until Stephanie said, "Well, it was nice talking to you. I'm sorry, I don't remember your name."

"Robert, Robert Covey. I enjoyed our conversation. Hopefully I'll get a chance to talk to you again."

Stephanie walked away without answering, but Robert knew he had her when she looked over her shoulder to see if he was watching her. Stephanie smiled and waved at Robert and he nodded his head in recognition. He saw her again two weeks later in the elevator. Stephanie was on her way up to see her father when Robert got on.

"How are you, Stephanie? You look—very nice today."

"Thank you, Robert."

"It's good to see you."

"It's good to see you again too, Robert." Stephanie was about to get off the elevator, when Robert stopped her.

"Wait a second, Stephanie."

Stephanie stopped and looked back at him. "I'm not going to take up a lot of your time. I just wanted to know if you had any plans for Saturday."

"Nothing I can't get out of." Stephanie smiled, and Robert almost forgot what he was going to say. "Why?"

"Would you like to get together, go to the park? Have a little picnic?"

"Sounds like fun, Robert," Stephanie said in a cool manner, but he could see the enthusiasm in her eyes. Robert smiled and Stephanie returned it. "Where?"

"Piedmont Park."

"What time?"

"You choose."

"Six too late?"

"No," Robert responded eagerly. "Six is fine. What would you like to eat?"

"Anything, I'm not fussy."

That was fifteen years ago, and from that day they were inseparable. Most people thought Robert was an opportunist, and was only with her because of what she could do for him, but that was not the case. He was so into Stephanie that he couldn't move left or right without discussing the ramifications with her first, and it was the same for her. They were married a year later, and for the next seven years they were very happy. And over that time, Robert worked hard and Stephanie worked behind the scenes, guiding his rise to director of research and development.

When Robert became a director, everything changed. He was always busy and his new position required him to do a lot more traveling. Over the next few years, his relationship with Stephanie became strained. It had gotten to the point where they barely saw each other. Stephanie said that she understood, but it slowly took its toll on the marriage.

It was Stephanie's idea for Robert to hire a personal assistant. It was her feeling, she said to him, that if he had somebody to "handle your light work," then he would have more time to spend with her. But Robert fell in love with Angela the minute she walked through the door, but the affair didn't begin right away. It took five years to develop. In spite of how he felt about her, Robert didn't go right at Angela. Despite the problems they were having, he still loved Stephanie and wanted to work things out with her. Besides, Robert thought that it was a mistake to get involved with people that he worked with.

For a while after hiring Angela, everything worked out the way Stephanie had intended. Angela was truly a godsend. Robert was home more often, and for a time, things got better, but it didn't last. Too much had gone on and too much had been said.

Robert and Angela got together the night that Anthony Marley had beaten Robert out for the position of vice president of operations. Angela burst through the door. "I don't believe this," she said, obviously disappointed by the news.

"I guess you heard," Robert said calmly.

"Do you believe this?"

"Are you pissed about something, Angela? 'Cause I'm sensing a bit of hostility coming from you."

"Damn right I'm pissed. Anthony is an idiot."

"Blithering idiot."

"Right, and a kiss-ass."

"That's why he's got the job." Robert smiled at Angela. "Maybe you're not kissing the right ass, Angela," he said with a hint of sarcasm.

"What are you trying to say, Robert?"

"Lighten up, Angela. All I'm saying is the boy is Brandon's brother. I don't know what we were thinking. The job was his from the start."

"I guess you're right," Angela sadly admitted.

"I'll see you in the morning."

"Where are you going?"

"I'm going to get drunk and pass out in some woman's arms," Robert said jokingly, but the thought had occurred to him.

"Wait a minute." She jumped up and followed Robert out of the office. "Mind if I go with you?" She smiled and looked him up and down. "I need a nice stiff one myself."

"Sounds like you're volunteering for the job."

"You never can tell, I just might be."

When they arrived at the bar, Robert and Angela sat down at the first empty table they could find. It just happened to be in a dark corner. "What are you drinking, Robert?" Angela asked as the waitress approached.

"Rémy Martin. Straight up with a water back and a twist of lemon."

"What's that?"

"What, Rémy? It's cognac. It's good stuff."

"I'll have one too," Angela said. She was still clearly shaken by today's events. "If you had gotten the job, I could have dealt with that. You've been doing the job for months. But Anthony, my God, he's only useful if you don't know where the party is. We went partying one night and he knew all the spots. But he is such a jerk. So full of himself I almost gagged. Now I work for this asshole. I know he's gonna be all over me now."

"Why is that?"

"I just know how he is, that's all."

"He wants you. Every man wants you, Angela," Robert said as if it were a matter of fact.

Angela looked at Robert and smiled to herself,

wondering if that included him. When the waitress returned with their drinks, Robert reached for his. "Don't go anywhere," he said. Then he turned up his glass and drank it like water. "Make the next one a double."

Angela followed suit, then grabbed her glass of water. "That burns a little going down."

Robert laughed. "For future reference, this is sipping liquor."

"I can tell you right now, there is no future in that drink for me. Bring me a sloe screw against the wall."

"A what?" Robert asked.

"It's a combination of a sloe gin fizz, a screwdriver, and a Harvey wall banger. It's good, you should try one."

"Nah, I try never to change horses in the middle of the stream."

Angela leaned forward and smiled alluringly at him. "Suppose the horse throws you off. Do you mount the other horse and ride?"

"Maybe. But only if the horse knew I was just there for the ride."

Angela leaned back in her chair. The bluntness of his answer put her off, but only for a minute. She knew she had set the tone by picking up on his "pass out in some woman's arms" line. *Decide now*, Angela thought. Could she fuck Robert and work with him in the morning? She decided to back off the obvious flirtation and talk about something else. "That's how they did you. They just rode you, knowing all the while Anthony was their boy." Angela managed to turn sexual innuendo into something work related. Robert admired her for her ingenuity.

For the next few hours, and four more doubles, Robert and Angela talked. After her fourth screw against the wall, Angela was in a mode he wasn't accustomed to seeing her in. She had taken off her jacket and unbuttoned the top button. The second worked itself loose from her laughter. She didn't seem to care. Gone was the smooth and highly polished Angela, the personal assistant that she portrayed in the office. However, now, under the influence of alcohol, her naturally aggressive tendencies seemed more predatory, more sexual. Robert liked aggressive, powerful women. It was one of his weaknesses. He looked Angela over; with her blouse unbuttoned, she exposed just enough of her cleavage to make him notice. More cleavage than he had given her credit for. His other weakness was cleavage, and he wondered if she was wearing a bra. Angela was a very attractive woman. She kissed him on the cheek. "What was that for?"

"'Cause I felt like it." She smiled. "I wanted to see if I'd like it. I was aiming for your lips, but you turned your head too quick."

Since she was a little too drunk to drive, Robert took Angela home. She slept on the way to her house, and had sobered up by the time they got there. She invited Robert in for a nightcap.

"What should we drink to?"

"I don't know, anything, so long as it doesn't involve Anthony or anything work related," Robert replied, and stepped toward Angela.

"Let's drink to this evening. I had a really nice time tonight."

"I'll drink to that. I enjoyed the evening too."

"Do you mean that?" Angela said, almost in disbelief. "I never got the impression that you liked me very much."

"Why? Because I'm not all over you like everybody else?"

"No, actually I appreciate you not being all over me. I think it's inappropriate for a work environment. There I go talking about work. Anyway, here's to tonight. I enjoyed your company."

Robert and Angela toasted their evening and emptied their glasses. He leaned forward to put his glass on the bar just as Angela reached for the bottle to refill the glasses. Her breasts brushed softly against his chest, ending all speculation about whether she was wearing a bra. "I mean that, Robert, I like the way you carry yourself. Strictly business. I watch the way you handle yourself. The way you dress. The way you walk. It's very sexy." Angela handed Robert his glass and stepped to his chest again. She exhaled. He felt her nipples brush his chest.

"I didn't know you watched me that closely," Robert replied, trying to sound unimpressed, but failing.

"That's because you don't pay me any attention."

"You're wrong. I notice quite a bit about you, Angela." His eyes met hers, then dropped to her cleavage. Angela touched his face and he kissed her.

Chapter 11

When Robert came into the apartment, his first thought was to call Angela to let her know that he was back and that he was all right. He knew that she had to be worried about him after not hearing from him for two days. He sat down at his desk and had just reached for the phone when it rang. "Hello."

"Robert Covey?" asked a man with a foreign accent that sounded Middle Eastern.

"Yes. Who is this?"

"I'm a friend of a friend."

Robert laughed a little. "I have a lot of friends, some good, and some bad. Some I like, and some I don't like. Could you be more specific?"

"I'm a friend of Floyd Dorsey."

Robert sat up straight in his chair. "What can I do for you?"

"I believe you have something for me."

"I don't know what you're talking about."

"I had a deal with Mr. Dorsey. He was supposed to deliver a package to me, but I never received it."

"Once again, I don't know what you're talking about. Why don't you ask Floyd about this package whatever it is?"

"Don't play games with me, Mr. Covey. You know exactly what I'm talking about. I had a deal with Mr. Dorsey. You, Mr. Covey, were his partner. You and I both know that Mr. Dorsey is dead. Now stop fucking around and tell me when I'm going to receive what was promised to me."

"Look, Dorsey is dead, and as far as I'm concerned, the deal died with him. Why don't we leave it at that?"

"I don't think you understand, Mr. Covey. Mr. Dorsey may be dead but the deal is still very much alive. I know that you know how serious a matter this is, and what steps I am willing to go through to get what I want."

"Quite the contrary, actually. I understand fully what you are willing to do to get what you want. But I don't think you understand that Dorsey is dead, and whatever it is that he was supposed to give you died with him."

"You are trying my patience, Mr. Covey. So let me make it plain to you. You are going to give me what I want."

"How many times do I have to say this? I don't have it and I don't know where it is."

"Find it, Mr. Covey."

"I don't think so."

"Quite the contrary, Mr. Covey. I think that you will find it, and you will bring it to me, or you will suffer the same fate as your wife."

"What? What did you say?"

"I see I have your attention now. The time for games is finished. I have been in that apartment, so I know that you have caller ID. Call me back when you have the package," the man said, and ended the call.

Robert checked the phone to be sure that he actually had the number, then he called Stephanie's apartment. When he got no answer, he tried calling her at their house. Once again he got no answer.

Robert got up and began pacing around the room. The man said that he would suffer the same fate as Stephanie, but what fate was that? He walked back to the phone and started to call the old man, but thought better of it since Brandon Marley wasn't well. "Who? Who could I call?"

Robert returned to his desk and picked up the telephone again. While the phone rang, he thought that if anything happened to Stephanie because of what he had gotten involved in he would never be able to forgive himself. Even though he and Stephanie had grown apart, largely because of his relationship with Angela, there was a time when he had loved Stephanie very deeply.

"Hello," Anthony Marley answered.

"Anthony, this is Robert. Sorry to be calling you so late—"

"You got a lot of nerve calling here," Anthony said angrily.

"I'm looking for Stephanie and I can't get in touch with her."

"Why did you call here, Robert? Is this some kind of sick joke? If it is, it's not funny, Robert."

"Did something happen to Stephanie?"

"You know exactly what happened to her. Stephanie is dead, Robert."

"Oh God, no." Robert's hand began to shake and he almost dropped the phone. "When—what happened? Did she have an accident?"

Anthony could hear the shock and horror in his voice, and his tone softened. "You didn't know."

"No, I've been fishing with Kiel Rhodes for a couple days. I just got back in town a few minutes ago."

"Oh. I'm sorry to have to tell you this, but Stephanie was murdered two days ago and the police and the FBI are looking for you."

"Me—they think I killed her?"

"Where are you, Robert?"

"I'm—I gotta go, Anthony," Robert said quickly, and hung up the phone.

Robert sat there, staring at nothing in particular. He knew that there was no way that he couldn't give Floyd's contact the package. Robert also knew that if he didn't, Angela might be the next one they went after to make him cooperate. He grabbed the phone and dialed Angela's number, but quickly ended the call.

If the police and the FBI were looking for him for Stephanie's murder, then they might have some type of surveillance on Angela hoping that it would lead to him. That meant that going to her house was definitely out of the question. His mind began to race, his heart began beating faster, and his breathing became labored. He had to get out of there, get some air. Robert grabbed his keys and rushed out the door.

He got in his car, rolled down all the windows, and sped out into traffic, almost causing an accident. He didn't know where he was going; he just drove and thought about what he had done. It didn't matter that he didn't do it himself; he was responsible for Stephanie's death.

When he was finally able to calm himself down and got himself together, Robert began thinking about what he was going to do next. He figured that as long as they thought he was going to give them what they wanted, Angela would be safe. That would at least buy him some time, but he knew that time was something that he didn't have much of. Robert had to do whatever he had to do to keep Angela safe.

Chapter 12

While Robert thought about Angela's safety, Angela thought about how Robert could betray her. How could he say that he loved her and set for up for Floyd's murder? How could she be in love with a murderer?

Angela thought back to the call Robert got before he sent her to see Floyd. At the time, she didn't think anything of it, but now Angela remembered walking into his office to get his signature and Robert was on the phone. When she came in, he immediately spun around in his chair and began whispering.

"Oh, I'm sorry. I'll come back," Angela said to Robert that afternoon.

Robert held up one hand to let her know that he wanted her to wait. Not that she was trying to eavesdrop, but Angela couldn't make out what he was saying, and now she wished she had. "That can't happen," she had heard him say. Then, "I understand. I'll take care of it."

After Robert hung up the phone, he spun around and practically jumped out of the chair.

"I didn't mean to interrupt you," Angela said when Robert hung up. "But I just wanted to give you these to papers to sign before you left for your meeting with Floyd." She thought about the look on his face. Angela had worked with Robert long enough to know that there was something bothering him. But once again, she had thought nothing of it, and once again she wished she had.

"There's been a change in plans, Angela. I need you to do something important for me."

"What do you need me to do?" Angela remembered asking without questioning what happened to change his plans. Now, in retrospect, Angela could see how she had allowed her feelings for Robert to compromise her better judgment.

"I want you to go with me to meet Floyd."

Angela's face contorted. "Me? Why? You know I can't stand to be in the same room with him."

"I know that, and wouldn't ask you to do this, but it's important. There's something not quite right about this deal. Something that Floyd is not telling me. I need to know what it is."

After Robert explained that he wanted her to go in alone and get Floyd talking and that he would be in the next office listening, Angela reluctantly agreed.

On the way to Floyd's office, there was very little conversation between the two. Before she went in, Robert grabbed her hand. "Thank you, Angela. I love you."

"I love you too," Angela said that day and went to meet Floyd. Now she wondered if Robert really killed both Floyd and Stephanie and left her to take the blame.

"How could I have been so stupid, Marcus?"

"Not stupid, Angela. Just in love and willing to do whatever was needed."

"What am I going to do now? I didn't have anything to do with any of this."

"How did Robert get involved with Floyd?"

"Robert met Floyd when they were both negotiating with the Defense Department for the contract we'd worked on. After that, Floyd told Robert about a stock scam that he could make money on. It's been on between them ever since."

"Stock scam? Tell me about that."

Angela stood up. "I could use a drink. What about you?"

"Are you trying to get me drunk?"

"Yes. And then I plan on seducing you," Angela said in her sexiest voice. Then she started to laugh, picked up his glass, and then stopped suddenly. "You do know that I was kidding, right?"

During the time that they had spent together, she had been thinking back to their days in college. The time that she and Marcus had spent together, and how she enjoyed being with him. Marcus was a very attractive man. He was the kind of man she wanted in her life, a man like Robert. She wondered about the choices she had made and how those choices had shaped her life and how they had led her to the situation that she found herself in.

Angela wondered how her life would have been different if she had given in to her feelings for Marcus. Feelings that she had denied to herself. She wondered what it would be like if she gave in to those feelings now.

"I know, but I'd still like that drink," Marcus said, quietly wishing that she wasn't, but at the same time, glad that she was only kidding. "So, what kind of stock scam were Robert and Floyd involved in?"

"The way Robert explained it to me was through some kind of dummy company, they buy stock that traded for small change."

"Small change?"

"They're usually stock offerings from smaller companies. Say for example that XYZ Corporation stock is selling for ten cents a share. For a hundred thousand dollars they can buy a million shares."

"So now they own a million shares of practically worthless stock. I don't get it."

"What happens next is that they buy an e-mail list and send a mass mailing to people who buy stock. The e-mail says, 'Hey, XYZ Corporation is about to merge with some bigger company.' Or something like that to let the reader know that the stock is getting ready to take off, and all but promising big returns. You gotta remember the people receiving these e-mails are used to getting stock tips via e-mail all the time."

"So they buy the stock 'cause it's so cheap. But I still don't get how it works. That seems to be more of a way for XYZ to raise capital."

"Sometimes the companies are involved for that

reason. But since it's such a cheap gamble, with big potential, people buy and the stock price goes up. So now in less than a week XYZ is trading at forty cents a share. Now your stock is worth four hundred thousand dollars."

"Now I understand. They sell that stock and make a quick three-hundred-thousand-dollar profit."

"You give somebody twenty-five thousand dollars and a week later they hand you two hundred thousand, so you tend to want to be in on the next deal they offer you."

"So is that what this is about, another stock scam?"

"I wish I could tell you, so you could stop asking me the same damn question," Angela said, and let go a deep yawn.

Marcus looked at his watch. "I didn't realize that it was this late." He drained his glass. "I think I've beat up on you enough for one night."

"I am not going to argue with you. You *are* my lawyer," Angela said, and thought about making a move to turn the conversation, but then she thought better of it. Marcus didn't seem to be interested in her, just in helping her with her situation. But she wanted to, she wanted Marcus, and wondered if it was just because she felt Robert had betrayed her.

"And as your lawyer I say we call it a night. But call me anytime if anything happens or if you think of anything that might be helpful." Marcus stood up. "Or if you just need to talk. I promise not to be your lawyer all weekend."

"Thank you, I might just do that."

"If not you call me Monday and let me know what's good for you. We still have a lot to talk about, Angela."

Angela stood and walked up to Marcus. "I know, really. You have pointed that out in excruciating detail," she said, looped her arm in his, and walked him to the door. She felt a rush of warmth being that close to him. Marcus felt it too, but neither acted on this feeling.

While he drove Marcus thought about his evening with Angela. How at one point in his life he would have given anything for a night alone with her just talking. When they were in college, he used to imagine that Angela would call him late one night and ask him to come to her room. That Angela would confess that she was secretly in love with him, and he would share his secret love for her. He had come a long way from there to being glad that she was kidding about wanting to seduce him.

When Marcus made it to his house, he took off his jacket as soon as he closed the door. He dropped it on the couch and went into his office to check his messages, loosening his tie as he walked. While he listened to his messages, Marcus glanced over at the pile of mail that he hadn't opened and decided he would get to it in the morning. His plan for the evening was to take a shower and relax. He got up thinking that he needed to put thoughts of Angela and everything else she was going through to the side and enjoy a much-needed weekend off. Marcus turned on the lights in his bedroom and was overwhelmed by what he saw.

Marcus looked around the room and walked in slowly. It was in shambles; everything was turned over and on the floor, and then he saw the bed. Whoever ransacked the room had cut the bed to shreds with a knife. There were pieces of the bed, sheets, and the pillow all around the room.

In that instance, Marcus wondered if whoever did it was still in the house. Suddenly he felt cold as fear washed over him. Marcus backed out of the room slowly and went into his office. He took his gun out of the metal case that he kept it in, dialed 911, and then called Garrett.

While Marcus waited for them to get there, he thought about who would do something like this to him. He didn't keep any valuables or cash in the house, so he didn't think it was a robbery. He thought about what the officer had told him the night before. "May have just been some kids playing a prank." If that were the case, maybe he got home before they had a chance to search the house. But why cut up the bed? Or maybe it was some client that he'd defended that was found guilty and blamed Marcus. "Or maybe it's Panthea."

He thought about the last time he saw her. It was an overcast Sunday afternoon and Marcus was in his office at the house preparing for court the next morning, when the doorbell rang. He started to ignore it and keep working, but he needed to take a break so he got up to see who it was. First, Marcus looked out the window, but didn't see any car in the driveway. Then he went to the door and looked through the peephole, and once again saw nobody.

When he opened the door, there stood Panthea, wearing nothing but four-inch stilettos and a smile.

"What the hell is wrong with you?" Marcus yelled and looked around to see if any of his neighbors could see her. What Marcus didn't know was that she had come to the door with a coat on, but when she heard Marcus unlock the door, Panthea quickly dropped the coat to the ground and kicked it out of sight.

"Aren't you going to invite me in?" Panthea smiled.

His first thought was to close the door in her face and get back to work, but he didn't. He grabbed her by the arm and pulled her into the house.

The moment he shut the door behind them, Panthea's lips covered his. She bit at his lip, sucked his tongue, and started trying to take his clothes off. Marcus pushed her off, but Panthea pushed back and stroked his erection.

"Stop," Marcus managed.

"You don't mean that, Marcus. You know you want me, baby," Panthea told him as she unzipped his pants and fell to her knees. Marcus looked down at her and watched as she took him into her mouth. Even though he hated to admit it, he did want her and a naked woman was very hard to resist.

Marcus grabbed Panthea's shoulders and carefully pulled her up. "You can't keep doing stuff like this. It has to stop. You can't just show up here naked."

"That's not exactly true, since that's exactly what I did."

Marcus shook his head. "How did you get here?"
When she didn't answer, he said, "Let me get you
something to put on and I'll take you home."

"Look, Marcus, I know you're tired of me, and
you don't want to be with me. I get it. I don't like
it but I get it. So I'll make you a deal."

"What's that?"

"You fuck me right here, right now, and you'll
never see me again," Panthea said as she stroked
his still hard erection. "You knock my back out this
one last time and I will be out of your life forever."

Before Panthea could say another word, Marcus
turned her around, bent her over the couch, and
shoved himself inside her. Panthea wiggled her
hips until he was right where he needed to be. She
rocked her hips, so he could hit her spot.

Panthea looked at him over her shoulder, and
grinned at him wickedly. Panthea closed her eyes
and gave in to the feeling. She moved her hips, still
rocking, as he squeezed her breasts from behind.

Panthea felt her nipples stiffen as they bounced
into the cushion. When Marcus spanked her thigh,
the sensation turned her on even more. The sound
of him sliding in and out of her filled her with
desire.

Marcus grabbed her by the shoulders and pulled
her body into his. Panthea started twisting her hips
and worked her way back up to a standing position.

"Oh God, Marcus, yes!" she cried. He started rubbing her thighs and her ass at the same time. Then he
stopped and took a few steps back. He wondered
what the hell he was doing. This would only make

things worse, he thought. Even though he loved fucking Panthea, loved her, being inside her would only make her think she could do it all the time. *And what would be the harm in that?* Marcus asked himself, and considered softening his position.

She turned around, and watched Marcus stroking his length, and she wondered why he had stopped. Panthea rubbed her hands over her breasts. She ran her hands up to her neck and back down to her stiff and very sensitive nipples. Then she squeezed them between her fingers. Without a word, Panthea fell to her knees and took Marcus into her mouth again.

The sensation was incredible and the feeling overwhelmed him. "Damn," Marcus shrieked and stumbled back onto a nearby chair.

Panthea shook her hips and breasts to the music she heard in her mind. She stepped to him, spread her legs wide, and moved her breasts to his face.

With his tongue, he glazed her nipple. He had his eyes open, watching Panthea watching him as he suckled her nipple. Panthea watched as his tongue moved around the chocolate-covered raisins, then slopped her entire breast. She began playing with the other one. Marcus pulled back and started watching her.

"You like what you see?" she asked, moving her hands between her thighs.

Marcus didn't answer with words. He palmed her breasts and squeezed again. Panthea put her hand on his shoulder to steady herself, and swung one leg over and mounted him.

Panthea started shaking her hips and rubbing her

breasts again. Taking a finger into her mouth, she traced from her lips, to her chin, then down to her neck and then to her belly button.

As Panthea bounced up and down on him, she twisted her hips, rocked them from left to right. Then she spread her legs even farther apart, and bent her knees slightly and started to shake her ass up and down on his length.

Marcus held Panthea close and gyrated his hips, in perfect sync with her rhythm. He could feel her walls tightening and loosening around him.

"You love this pussy, don't you?" Panthea said as she rotated between a bounce and a grinding move that seemed to bring him immense pleasure.

"Yeah, that's it, come for me," Panthea instructed. "I want to feel you explode inside me."

Marcus moved his hips, and tried to pump himself into her as hard as he could from his position. Panthea matched his every move stroke for stroke. She felt him begin to expand inside her, and she picked up her pace and started gyrating her hips even faster and harder. He grabbed her waist and tried to slow her movement, but it did little good. Soon their screams of passion filled the room and they collapsed in each other's arms.

When it was over, Panthea admitted that her coat was outside and her car was parked down the street. With a tear rolling down her face, she kissed Marcus on his cheek and left the house.

Since that day, more than two months ago, he hadn't seen or heard from her. Marcus didn't think Panthea was capable of doing something like this, and didn't think that after all this time she'd do this, but there was no way for him to be sure. He asked Garrett to check on her after what had happened the night before, but with everything else going he could understand if he hadn't gotten around to it yet.

When the police arrived, once again they checked the house to be sure that nobody was in there, and then proceeded to collect whatever evidence that they could find in all that mess. While that was going on, Marcus spoke to a detective. "As far as you can tell there is nothing missing from the residence, is that correct?" the detective asked as he took notes.

"Not that I can tell," Marcus said.

"You have any idea who might do something like this?"

"I have some ideas, but I'd rather not speculate. Let's wait and see what your men come up with inside first."

"Fair enough," the detective said, and went to join the crime scene technicians, as Garrett came speeding into the driveway.

"You all right?"

"Yeah, Garrett, I'm fine. Thanks for coming."

"What the fuck is goin' on, big dawg?"

"The other night when I got home, I found the door open. Then, twice last night somebody, I don't know if it was a man or a woman, called and held the phone, but didn't say anything. And then tonight somebody broke in again and ransacked my bedroom and cut up my bed with a knife."

"Somebody took a knife to your bed and you don't know if it's a man or a woman?"

"You know what I mean, Garrett."

"You have any idea who it could be?"

"I know you been busy running around for me, but have you had a chance to check on Panthea Daniels yet?"

"You think she did this?"

"I don't think so, but I really don't know. That's why I need you to take a run at her."

"I'm on it first thing tomorrow morning. In the meantime, I don't think you should stay in that house tonight."

"I don't think that's necessary, Garrett. Just check on Panthea for me."

"Okay, let's just say for a minute that it's not Mrs. Daniels, and it's some mad-crazy ex-client, fresh out of prison, who spent years thinking about how he was going to terrorize and then torture you to death."

"You have a point."

"I'm glad that you see that." Garrett reached in his pocket, pulled out his keys, and threw them to Marcus. "Look, I'm with the kids this weekend, so why don't you stay at my place for the weekend?"

"That's all right, Marcus. I'll check into a hotel for the night. I'll give you a call in the morning."

Garrett laughed. "Too good to stay at my little rinky-dink apartment?"

"No, it's not that," Marcus started to explain.

"I'm just kiddin' with ya, big dawg. I'll talk to you in the morning." Marcus tried to hand him back the keys. "Hang on to them, just in case you change your mind."

Marcus drove downtown and checked into a room at the Westin Peachtree Plaza Hotel. After having a couple of drinks at the bar, he went upstairs and went to sleep.

At 2:45 A.M., Marcus was awakened as the phone rang, but again no one was on the line. Now Marcus was wide-awake and concerned about whether he had a stalker. So concerned that he couldn't go back to sleep.

He got out of bed and got a drink out of the minibar. He thought about the calls he got the night before and wondered if it would happen again. Marcus sat up watching the clock, waiting for five o'clock.

When the phone rang at exactly 5:00 A.M., a female voice said, "You can't hide from me."

"Who is this?"

"You didn't think you could just throw me away and move on to the next one."

"What are you talking about? Who is this?"

"Oh, I'm nothing, I'm nobody. So don't worry, after a while I'll go away and you can go back to your normal life and your new BMW and your big house. Oh yeah, I forgot, you don't have a house to go home to."

"What? What do you mean?"

"Go home and see."

Marcus hung up the phone, got dressed, and drove to his house. He got there just in time to find the firemen had just gotten finished putting out the fire.

Chapter 13

Once the fire was put out and the fire crew had left the scene, Marcus spoke with an arson investigator that explained to him that the fire was set using gasoline, which was spread throughout the house. "Definitely arson, Mr. Douglas."

After he left, Marcus spent the rest of the morning with a police detective, talking about his ex-wife and his ex-girlfriends. He told them about the early morning phone calls that he'd been receiving and what the caller said to him.

"Did you recognize the voice, Mr. Douglas?" the detective asked.

"No, I couldn't. All I could tell is that it was a woman's voice, but it was muffled. Like she had something over the receiver."

"I understand. When you left here after the last incident, where did you go?"

"I drove downtown and checked into the Westin."

"Did you stop anywhere, or talk to anybody?"

"No, sir, not on the way there, but I did go to the

bar in the hotel. I had a couple of drinks and then went to my room."

"You talk to anybody at the bar?"

"Other than the bartender, no."

"Was anybody else at the bar?"

"Yes, there were a few people there."

"Did you recognize anybody?"

"No."

"Did you notice anything, or see anybody watching you, while you were at the bar?"

"No, at least not that I paid any attention to. I was just trying to clear my head."

"How long were you at the bar?"

"Maybe forty-five minutes, no more than an hour. Like I said, I really wasn't paying much attention to anything."

"After the night you had I can't say I'd have been any more observant under the circumstances." The detective put away his notes. "What I think happened is that your stalker was somewhere close by and followed you to the hotel."

"That was my thought as well."

"I guess you didn't see anybody following you?"

"No."

"I have officers canvassing the area. I'll make sure they are aware that she may still be in the area."

"For all we know she may be watching us right now."

"It's a strong possibility."

"Great."

When he left the police, Marcus was tired from not sleeping much the night before. He considered going to another hotel, but was afraid that if his stalker was still in the area she, whoever she was, would follow him and the same thing would happen again. "She already burned down the house, what else can she do?" As he got in his car, Marcus paused and thought about the question he had just asked himself. "She could kill you this time."

Marcus started up the car and drove away from what used to be his house. For the next hour, he drove around, looking in his rearview mirror. He thought about calling Garrett and taking him up on his offer to use his apartment, but Garrett was with his kids and Marcus didn't want to take any more time away from them than he already had.

While he drove, Marcus thought back to something Panthea had said when they first met. "The Ferguson trial," she told Marcus that first day in his office. "I used to watch you on the news every night before I went to bed."

"You're not about to start stalking me, are you, Mrs. Daniels?" he remembered asking playfully.

"Please, call me Panthea, and no, I'm not a stalker. Besides, I always thought that stalking referred to *unwanted* attention or contact."

"You are stating that I'm going to want your attention and contact?"

"I'm not saying anything like that, Mr. Douglas. I was just trying to define what you meant by stalking."

The idea that Panthea was the one who was stalking him made sense. He thought about what the woman said, *You didn't think you could just throw me away and move on to the next one.* She was the last woman that he was involved with, and he could see why she might feel like he had thrown her away. But he hadn't picked up with any other woman since then. Yeah, there was the occasional stray, but no one serious, and certainly not on the level of the relationship that he had with Panthea. At one point before he found out the truth about what she had done, he was very much in love with her. "Or maybe I was just pussy-whipped," Marcus said aloud as he continued to drive.

Before he knew it he was in Angela's neighborhood. He hadn't intended to go there, but there he was. There were still a lot of things that he didn't understand about her situation, things he would need to know if he was going to help her. He still believed that there was something that Angela wasn't telling him about Robert Covey and Floyd Dorsey, and Marcus also needed to know what she knew about Chuck Prentice's murder.

Since he was sure that nobody was following him, Marcus decided to go by there. Now, in addition to her issues, it was he that could use an old friend to talk to. He parked his car and walked to the door, hoping that it wasn't too early for her, or that she was alone. "Maybe Robert showed up there. Which wouldn't necessarily be a bad thing. Then we could get some answers."

Marcus rang the bell and waited. It didn't take long before Angela came to the door. "Who is it?"

"It's Marcus, Angela."

"Let me put something on."

"Don't go to any trouble on my account," Marcus said quietly, and allowed himself to slip into the fantasy of seeing Angela naked.

Five minutes later, Angela opened the door, wearing jeans and an old college sweatshirt. "Good morning, Marcus. Come on in," she said, in a cheery manner that made Marcus feel even more tired than he already was.

"Sorry to just drop by again like this, but—"

"I know, you find me absolutely irresistible and you can't stay away from me," Angela mused.

Marcus smiled and laughed a bit. "Yeah, that's it," he said, thinking how at one time how true that was.

"You look tired, Marcus. You all right?"

"I'm okay. I just didn't get much sleep last night."

"Up all night thinking about me and my problems, no doubt. You always were driven that way, dedicated. I always admired that about you. Once you're on to something, you don't let go until you get it."

"Admired me, huh?" Marcus thought for a second about telling her how he had felt about her during those days, but the feeling passed quickly. "But that's not what kept me up all night."

Marcus went on to recap his early morning activities, and that he had somebody stalking him. All Angela could say was, "Whaat? You're kidding, right?"

"I wish I were."

"Do you think it was a good idea for you to come here? Suppose this nut comes here looking for you?

I have enough going on to have to be bothered with some crazy woman that thinks something is going on between us," Angela said, glad that she hadn't tried to seduce him before he left her the night before.

"I don't think that will happen. I've been driving around for hours and I'm sure that nobody was following me here. So I think you'll be safe."

"Okay," Angela said tentatively. "If you say so. Have you eaten anything?"

"No, I haven't eaten anything since lunch yesterday."

"Why don't you have a seat, and I'll make us some breakfast?"

"Thank you, Angela. I'd like that."

After breakfast, Angela insisted that Marcus get some sleep in one of the other bedrooms in the house. Marcus took a shower and went to sleep.

When Marcus woke up it was getting dark. He wandered through the house and found Angela sitting on her deck watching the late summer sun set. "Hello," he said, and joined her on the deck.

"Well, hello, sleepyhead. I was beginning to think that you were going to sleep through until the morning."

"I guess I really needed the rest. Thank you for letting me pass out here." Marcus sat down in the chair next to Angela.

"So, what happens now?"

"Find someplace to live temporarily, and wait until the insurance company pays."

"Were they able to save anything?"

"Nothing. All I have are the clothes on my back and my car."

"I can't even imagine what that must feel like. I mean, not only to have somebody stalking you, but to lose everything."

"Funny, I was thinking the same thing about you and your situation. You wanna trade places?"

Angela laughed. "Some nut stalking me or life in prison for a crime I didn't commit. Under normal circumstances I would say yes, you know, just to be polite. But you can own that one and I'll own mine."

"Thanks. That says a lot."

"Do you have any idea who it is?"

"I have some idea," Marcus said, and told Angela about Panthea and why he felt that he had to stop seeing her.

"I understand why you might feel that way. Truth and trust are important in any relationship, but I think you were wrong."

"What makes you say that?"

"You said that you were in love with her. If you really loved her, you could have worked through that."

"Love conquers all."

"That's oversimplifying it, but yes. If you really love somebody, that gives you someplace to start." Angela looked at Marcus and waited for him to comment. When he didn't she continued. "I could see why, feeling the way that you say she felt about you, she wouldn't want you to know that she'd accidentally killed somebody. And you proved her right, as soon as you found out the truth about what she had done and about the thing she had done in her past, you dropped her."

"But how would I ever know if she really loved me, Angela? I had to ask myself, was everything we shared all part of some plan? How would I know if Panthea made me fall in love with her so I would do whatever it took to acquit her?"

"I didn't say it would have been casy, I just said it would have given you someplace to start from."

Marcus looked at Angela. "I guess that explains why you are so willing to protect Robert."

"I guess it does. I love him. So whether I trust him or not, whether he killed Floyd and Stephanie, I still love him."

"What about Chuck Prentice?"

"What about him?"

"Did you know him?"

"Of course I knew Chuck. He was a lead programmer in our department," Angela said, and looked away, but looked back quickly.

"Do you think Robert killed Chuck?"

"I know that everybody in the office thinks that Robert had something to do with it."

"What do you think?"

Angela got up and leaned over the rail on her deck. "Robert knew that Chuck had a thing for Stephanie, and they did have a very public fight about it at the office, but that's not why Chuck was killed."

"Okay, why was Chuck killed?"

When Angela didn't answer right away, Marcus

got up and went to the rail and leaned next to her. "Why was Chuck murdered, Angela?"

"Whatever it is that Robert and Floyd were involved in, Chuck had a part in it, and that is what got him killed."

"Now we're getting somewhere. What were they involved in?"

"How many times do I have to say this? I don't know what they were into. And before you ask, I don't know where Robert is," Angela said angrily.

"Okay, Angela, I'm sorry. I don't mean to upset you. I just need to know what's going on here."

"I'm sorry too, Marcus. I know that you're just trying to help."

"Well, let me help you, Angela. You have got to start telling me the truth, or at least stop leaving things out. Now, what makes you say that Chuck was murdered because of whatever it was that Robert and Floyd were involved in?"

"That's what they were arguing about that night."

"Who, Robert and Floyd?"

"Yes. I told you that the night Floyd was murdered he and Robert were arguing. Robert said that what Floyd was doing was going to get them killed."

"I remember you said that Floyd told Robert that he had taken steps to make sure that wouldn't happen."

"Yes, but what he said was that he had taken steps to make sure that what happened to Chuck wouldn't happen to them."

"See what I mean about leaving things out?"

Angela smiled. "I see what you mean, and

I promise that I'm not going to leave anything else out."

"I think the best thing for us to do now is start over. Start at the beginning, Angela, and this time you have to tell me everything."

"I was afraid you were going to say that. You know that is the last thing I want to do tonight." Angela gave Marcus a look, and he wondered what she had in mind. "And what happened to you not being my lawyer this weekend? What happened to you just being a friend this weekend?"

"Somebody burned my house to the ground," Marcus said flatly. If he wanted to be honest with himself, he would have to admit that he was still very attracted to Angela. "But we don't have to talk about this if you don't want to, we can talk about or do whatever you want."

Angela smiled the smile Marcus had fallen in love with all those years ago. "What did you have in mind, Mr. Douglas?"

"Whatever you want, Ms. Pettybone."

Marcus needed to release some of the tension, and having sex with Angela would definitely accomplish that. It would be like a dream come true, one that he'd had for years. Marcus looked at Angela again. She was beautiful and her body was to die for. He looked away quickly when she looked at him. They had been quietly flirting with each other since they first saw each other, but for reasons of their own, each would back away before it went to the next level.

"But whatever you want to do, you might as well

get used to talking about this," Marcus said, once again finding a way to pull back on his desire to make love to Angela. "Because if things break against you and you're charged in any of these murders, we are going to go over this from start to finish more times than either of us can count. I know that you don't, but it would sure help if you knew where Robert was, and what he was doing."

Chapter 14

Robert walked to his car quickly and hoped that he wasn't seen. He had been in Floyd's office for over an hour, looking without success for the package that Floyd had promised his contact. "What now?" he said aloud as he got in the car. But Robert knew where he had to go next, though he was reluctant to go there. He would have to search Floyd's house.

If the police and the FBI were looking for him, there was a better than average chance that they would be watching the house. It was a chance that he knew he had to take. Angela's life might depend on him finding that package. Robert was still freaked out about Stephanie's death and his responsibility in it, and he refused to let Angela suffer the same fate.

As he drove he thought back to the day that this all began. The day he met Floyd Dorsey. Their two companies were competing for a contract to develop a portion of the Defense Department's new missile-guidance system.

It was a little more than two years ago, when Robert and his team were at the Pentagon in Washington, D.C. They had just finished their presentation and he was talking to Lieutenant Colonel Lacy DeVille when Floyd and his team came into the office.

"Robert, let me introduce you to Floyd Dorsey, of CLOS Information," Lieutenant Colonel DeVille said that afternoon, and turned to Floyd. "Floyd Dorsey, Robert Covey."

"Good to meet you, Mr. Covey. I've heard a lot of good things about the work you're doing over at Integrated."

"Thank you. I do the best that I can," Robert remembered replying. He wished that he could return the compliment, but he had never heard of Floyd or his company before that day, and now he wished he hadn't. But he could tell from the company's name, CLOS, which stood for Command to Line-Of-Sight, that they were in the same business and that they were here to do a presentation for the same contract. But since Robert had never heard of them and he knew that they had the inside track because of Brandon Marley's connections, he wasn't worried.

"So I guess that means that you are the guys to beat," Floyd said as he and Robert shook hands.

"In that case, I feel that it's only fair to warn you that our proposal is going to be hard to beat."

"I look forward to the competition," Floyd said that day, and followed the lieutenant colonel into the conference room to make his pitch.

Later that night, Robert was in the hotel bar

having a drink when Floyd walked up to him and sat down. "How did your presentation go?" Robert asked, and signaled for the bartender.

"I think it went very well," Floyd replied as the bartender dropped a bar napkin in front of him. "Scotch and water, please, and bring my friend here whatever he's drinking."

As the evening wore on the two got into a conversation about the contract and the differences in their proposals. "Our system vastly improves the coordination between the missile and the target to ensure the collision," Robert told him.

"How so?" Floyd wanted to know.

"I can't get into the details, for obvious reasons."

"Obviously."

"However, it has to do with the missile's line of sight between the launcher and the target by correcting any deviation of the missile in relation to this line."

"Our big splash is in the manual command to Line-Of-Sight. The target tracking and the missile tracking and controls are performed manually. The operator watches the missile's flight. Our signaling system commands the missile back into the straight line between the operator and the target."

"Typically," Robert said arrogantly, "that is only useful for slower targets where significant lead is not required. But as speeds have increased, the manual system is useless for most roles."

Floyd laughed a little. "You know your stuff, but we've improved our semimanual and semiautomatic command to line-of-sight so the target tracking is manual and the missile tracking and control is automatic. It's very effective against ground targets like tanks and bunkers."

"I think that automatic command to line-of-sight where the target tracking, missile tracking, and control are automatic is really the way to go," Robert said to him, not really wanting to say any more about their system and what it could do.

As expected, Integrated was awarded the contract and began work in its development right away. Robert was surprised to get a call from Floyd. He said that the company had moved him from California to the Atlanta area, so he could lobby for business on Air Mobility Mission Systems, which were developed by Lockheed Martin in Marietta, Georgia.

It wasn't that he had anything against Floyd, or didn't like him, but he and his team were very busy with the development of the guidance system and he really didn't have the time. However, as a matter of professional courtesy, Robert agreed to meet Floyd one night for dinner.

That night over dinner and drinks, the two developed a good relationship. Robert even promised to throw some work in Floyd's direction, work that Floyd handled personally and did a great job on, which paved the way for more work and a closer relationship between the two. Robert considered Floyd a friend.

So when Floyd came to him with an investment opportunity that was a guaranteed moneymaker, Robert was all ears.

"We set up a dummy company, and we buy stock in smaller companies. Then we buy an e-mail list and send a mass mailing to people who buy stock, recommending the stock. They buy and the stock price goes up, and we sell."

"Is this legal, Floyd?"

"There are no regulations against it. But I'll tell you this, I can just about guarantee that if you get in on this with me you'll walk away with a couple of hundred thousand dollars in your pocket."

"In that case, count me in."

Floyd was as good as his word, and in less than a week he handed Robert a check drawn on their dummy company for two hundred thousand dollars.

"We should do business like this more often," Robert said as he looked at the check.

"Well, if you like that, Robert, then maybe you'll be interested in something else that may be a little more lucrative."

"How little?"

"A million dollars."

"What is it? Another stock deal?"

"Not exactly. My company is looking to upgrade our missile guidance system. You know, to allow us to compete for future business in foreign markets."

"And?"

"I was hoping that you'd consider selling me the program that Integrated is going to deliver to the DOD."

"Out of the question," Robert said flatly.

"Why?"

"I'm not gonna sell you company secrets. It wouldn't be ethical."

"Look, Robert, I know that in spite of the fact that you're married to the boss's daughter, your career at Integrated is at a standstill. Too many powerful people working against you. You stepped on a lot of big toes over there."

"How do you know this?"

"I hear things. But despite how I came across the information, it remains a fact. You said so yourself, Robert, you're looking to go out on your own, start your own company. This is your chance to do just that. You don't owe those people at Integrated anything."

Knowing that Floyd was right about his situation at Integrated, Robert agreed to sell Floyd the program with some minor modifications for one million dollars.

Robert knew that for that to happen he would need to involve Chuck Prentice. Chuck was the lead programmer on the project and his involvement was crucial to the success of it, and would be just as crucial if he was going to make it work. Chuck had personally written key elements of the program and would be needed to adapt the program to Floyd's specifications. Chuck agreed to get in, and the work began. Now he wished he had never met Floyd or allowed his own greed to get the better of his judgment. Now Floyd was dead, Chuck was dead, and Stephanie was dead. All those deaths were on his hands.

Chapter 15

Robert drove around Floyd's neighborhood for a while, looking for anything he thought looked out of the ordinary. Like vans or people sitting in parked cars. Once he had satisfied himself that the area was clear and it was safe to approach the house, Robert parked his car two blocks away and walked to Floyd's house and broke in the back door.

After searching the house from top to bottom, a frustrated Robert left the house the way he entered it and made his way back to his car. As he walked, Robert tried to think of anyplace else that he could search for the program that he had delivered to Floyd. "The only other place I can think of is a safe-deposit box at his bank." Robert knew that he couldn't get in there even if he wanted to, and he didn't want to go there.

He would have to come up with another plan, and come up with it soon. Robert got in his car and drove away thinking about the day that Chuck came into his office and relayed his suspicions that something wasn't quite right about their deal with Floyd. It was the day after their argument over Stephanie.

"What do you want?" Robert asked that afternoon when Chuck walked into his office.

"It's not about me and Stephanie, if that's what you're thinking," Chuck said and closed the door behind him.

"Well then, say what you gotta say and get out."

"Look, Robert—" Chuck started, but Robert cut him off.

"I talked to Stephanie, Chuck."

Robert remembered how the expression on Chuck's face changed when he said that.

"When?"

"Last night."

"What did she say?" Chuck asked, and sat down.

"She told me everything." There was a long uncomfortable silence between the two friends. "We're friends, Chuck, and you fucked my wife. How could you do that to me?"

"To you? How could you do what you been doing to Stephanie?"

"What the fuck are you talking about?"

"I'm talking about you and Angela." Now it was the look on Robert's face that changed. He had thought that he and Angela had been so careful to conceal their relationship. "You've got your head too far up Angela's ass to know how obvious it is to everybody. Stephanie loved you, Robert. She gave you everything you ever wanted and you shit on her for Angela. Stephanie doesn't deserve what you've done to her. She's a good woman, and she was a good wife to you."

"Good enough a wife to fuck my friend."

"Well, she won't be your wife much longer. You two will be divorced and you and Angela can run off together and start this big company on the money you get from Floyd."

"Did you tell Stephanie about our deal with Floyd?"

"Of course not. Your secret is safe."

"What do you want, Chuck?"

"Nothing. I'm out, Robert. I don't want any part of this anymore."

"Why? Why all of a sudden do you want out?"

"Because it's wrong, Robert, that's why. But like I said your head is too far up Angela's ass to realize that. All you can see now is the money."

"Like you don't? I know what's happening here. You're fucking my wife and now you've got your eyes on this office."

"You really are stupid, Robert, you know that. You have no idea what's really going on here. I always thought you were smarter than this. Truth is I could have had your job months ago, but I didn't want it."

"Since I'm so stupid, why don't you tell me what's really going on?"

"While you were off playing true confessions with Stephanie, Floyd came to see me last night."

Robert sat up in his chair. He thought that he had an understanding with Floyd that only he would have any dealings with Chuck. It was a system of checks and balances that Robert insisted on to maintain control of things and protect himself if anything went wrong. "What did Floyd want?"

"He asked me to make some changes to the program that could have severe consequences."

"Like what?"

"The targeting system and the destruct system."

"What about them?"

"I didn't realize when he first discussed it with me last night. But afterward I thought about it, began thinking through what those enhancements, as he called them, would do. If you were to do a little work, a third party could potentially change the missile trajectory or destruct the missile in flight."

"You're sure of this?"

"As sure as I am of my name," Chuck said, and folded his arms across his chest.

Robert picked up the phone right away and dialed Floyd's number. He told Floyd that Chuck had informed him of the changes he wanted, and insisted that they all meet to discuss it. "What's the matter, Robert? You and Chuck want more money?"

"You just be at Silk on Peachtree in an hour," Robert demanded, and hung up the phone.

When Robert and Chuck arrived at Silk, the upscale pan-Asian restaurant was packed as it usually was with stylish young diners feasting on sizzling Kobe steaks, huge live Maine lobsters, and succulent Chilean sea bass. The restaurant was decorated with bamboo floors, beautiful walnut woodwork, a collage of glass and silk panels behind the bar. They ordered drinks at the bar and waited for

Floyd to arrive. It was almost two hours later when Floyd walked through the door.

"So, what seems to be the problem, gentlemen?" Floyd asked after the bartender brought his drink.

"First of all," Robert said angrily, "I thought we agreed that you would have no contact with Chuck. Now I find that you went behind my back and asked him to make modifications to the original program."

"Calm down, Robert. I needed to discuss some modifications to the program. You weren't available last night when I called. You weren't at home and your cell was turned off, so I went to Chuck. Nothing sinister about that, and surely nothing to get upset about."

"Then you should have waited. Those modifications weren't anything that couldn't have waited until today."

"You're right, Robert, they weren't and I should have waited and discussed them with you first, but I was anxious to get them started. I apologize and I promise it won't happen again. Is there anything else?"

"Chuck has some concerns about the modifications that you asked him to make."

"What concerns are those, Chuck?"

"To be completely honest with you, Floyd, I'm not at all comfortable with the changes you asked me to make and the effect that they will have on the targeting and the destruct systems."

"What about the changes has made you uncomfortable, Chuck? Because you didn't seem to have any issues with the modifications when we spoke last night. As I recall, I asked you specifically if you had any problems with making the enhancements and you said that you didn't. Now, after you talk to Robert you're not comfortable. So I'm wondering what happened to change that. Because it seems to me that this is nothing more than the two of you wanting more money."

"He's as big an asshole as you are," Chuck said, and looked at Robert. "Last night I didn't realize that with those so-called enhancements a third party could potentially change the missile's trajectory or destruct the missile in flight."

"So how much more do you want?" Floyd asked, without even bothering to address Chuck's concerns. To Robert, that spoke volumes. "What, you want me to double the money?"

"Triple," Robert said quickly, and Chuck's mouth dropped open.

"Done." Floyd drained his glass and stood up. "Are we done here?"

Chuck started to say something to Floyd, but Robert grabbed his hand. "I think so."

"Good. I'll expect the work done in the time that we discussed last night."

After Floyd left Silk, Robert turned to Chuck. "Let's get out of here."

Once they were out of the restaurant and in Robert's car, Chuck asked, "What the fuck just happened? The bastard didn't even bother to deny that that's what those changes will do."

"I know. Did you notice that he went straight

to the money, and he didn't even blink when I said triple?"

"Of course I did, Robert. I was sitting right next to you. Something is definitely not right about this. What do you think he's doing?"

"I don't know for sure. But I have a good idea."

"You thinking what I'm thinking?"

"If you're thinking 'terrorist,' then yes."

"We can't do this, Robert, no way we can do this, not even for three million dollars!" Chuck yelled.

"Don't you think I know that!" Robert yelled back. "But we need to be sure of what he's doing."

"Why? Why do we need to be sure? What else could it be? That mothafucka is going to sell that program to terrorists. And in case you didn't know, that's called treason!"

"Would you stop yelling, Chuck? I'm sitting right next to you. I know it's treason."

"This is bad. Fuck that. This is way beyond bad."

"I know."

"I'm willing to do a lot of things for money, but selling out my country is not one of them."

"And you think I would?"

"Honestly I don't know, Robert. Like I said, you have been acting funny lately."

"Angela's ass ain't that deep that I can't see that this is wrong."

"We should go to the police, or maybe the FBI."

"And tell them what? That we were about to sell out our country?"

"Yes!"

"No! We need to be sure that's what he's doing and find out who he's doing business with."

"Some towel-head mothafucka with deep pockets. We should go to the FBI right now."

"That sounds like a plan for making us roommates at Leavenworth or some shit-hole like that. No, we find out exactly what Floyd is doing and who's backing him and then we go to the FBI. At least then we'll have some leverage to bargain with. That may be the only thing that keeps us out of prison."

"Okay, you're right, that makes sense. So how do we find out?"

"When were you supposed to get those changes to him?"

"Day after tomorrow."

"Okay. Tomorrow you call Floyd and tell him that you wanna cut a side deal. No, tell him that since you did all the work you want me out."

"You think he'll buy that?"

"He's a greedy fuck, and now he thinks we are too. If he seems skeptical, tell him you're fuckin' my wife and you want me out of the way so you can take over."

"That was low, Robert."

"I know, and I'm sorry I said it. You and I have got to stick together now."

"Look, Robert, I never meant for it to happen."

"Save it. Just be good to her. Be a better man to Stephanie than I was, and we'll call it square."

The following night Chuck called Robert and told him that he followed Floyd and he met with two Arab men and that that was the last time he heard from him. It was two days later when Robert found out that Chuck's body was found in his car in the West End with two bullets in his brain.

Robert knew that he had sent Chuck to be killed, but he still felt that he needed to know exactly who and what Floyd was involved with before he went to the FBI.

That was why he sent Angela to see Floyd that night to try to get the information that Chuck had died trying to get.

By using Floyd's private entrance, he was able to slip into Floyd's office without being seen. Robert stood in the next room and listened as Angela did what he asked.

"Robert is getting cold feet is all I know. He thinks you don't know what you're doing," Angela told Floyd that night.

Robert heard Floyd laugh. "Seems like you're trying to get me to tell you about the particulars of our deal."

"I always told Robert that he couldn't get anything past you. You're too smart a man for that," Angela said in a voice that Robert thought was just for him.

"I can't tell you anything about what we have going, Angela. If Robert wanted you to know, he would tell you himself."

It was difficult for him to stand in the other room listening to the woman that he loved flirting with Floyd, but she was only there because he sent her.

Robert knew that Angela didn't like Floyd, couldn't stand to be in the same room with the man. In that moment, he realized that he loved Angela more than he had ever loved any woman before her. Then things started to get ugly.

"I would be willing to include you in what Robert and I have going, Angela," Floyd told her that night. "It would be worth a great deal of money to you."

"How much money?"

"That depends on how well you do what I need you to do."

"What would I have to do?"

"You're a very beautiful woman, Angela."

"Thank you, Floyd."

"But you know that. You've known for a very long time that I want you, Angela. I wonder why all of a sudden you are, shall we say, more receptive?"

"You're a businessman, you should understand why I was trying to maintain a professional and businesslike relationship between us. I have always found that it works out better that way."

"I see. And believe me, when I say that under normal circumstances I would agree with that policy. But you, Angela, are not a normal woman. You are an extraordinary woman, my dear. One that should be sought and worshiped for her beauty. If you were mine I could do things for you that no man ever could."

"As long as you understand and recognize me as, not just a woman, but a businesswoman who is interested in making money, then I'm confident that I could become even more, shall we say, receptive.

So why don't you tell me what I would have to do for you to include me?"

There was a long silence in the room, and Robert was left to wonder what was going on. And then Angela broke the silence. "What are you doing, Floyd?"

Followed by more silence. Then, "What do you think you're doing? Let me go."

At that point, Robert couldn't take it any longer. He burst into the room.

Chapter 16

"Tell me everything you can remember about the argument between Robert and Floyd," Marcus said.

"When Robert came into the room he—"

"Back up for just a second. What were the two of you talking about that made Robert come into the room at that point? Because from what you're telling me, it was going just the way he wanted it."

Angela dropped her head. "Floyd was trying to rape me. He had taken off his jacket and tie, and unbuttoned his shirt. Then he grabbed my arms, pulled me up from the chair I was sitting in, and forced me down on his desk."

"Oh," Marcus said, feeling a little awkward about asking. "He didn't hurt you, did he?"

"No, Robert grabbed him and pulled him off me before it went too far."

"How much, if any, do you think that incident played into Robert's going back to Floyd's office after he dropped you off?"

Angela didn't answer right away, instead she took another sip of her drink while she considered her answer. "It's hard to say, Marcus."

"I mean, the woman he loved is flirting with Floyd just the way he told you to, and about to get raped in the next room." Marcus paused. "That had to have some effect on him. At best it had to have changed the tone of the conversation."

"I think that should be obvious. Robert was furious when he came in there."

"Did they fight, struggle, what?"

"No, it didn't get to that point. Robert just pulled him off me, and said, 'What the fuck are you doing?'"

"What did Floyd say?"

"Nothing at first. I think he was more surprised that Robert was in the next room."

"Did Floyd pick up on the fact that you were only flirting with him to get information?"

"If he did, he didn't say it."

"Okay," Marcus said, and took a deep breath. "What was said after that got straightened out?" he asked, choosing not to mention that Angela had once again left out crucial information.

"Once everything had calmed down, Robert asked Floyd what was really going on. Floyd said he was trying to close a deal that would make them a lot of money. Robert said that he understood that, but things had changed since Floyd first came to him about doing the deal."

"What changed?"

"Chuck."

"What happened with Chuck?"

"By that time Chuck was dead."

"I know that. I need to know how Chuck fit into the deal."

"As I said," Angela started, then got up and began walking about the room as she talked. "Chuck Prentice was a lead programmer at our company, probably the best programmer on staff. If there was a tough project, Chuck was your man. Organization skills, attention to detail, I don't think there would be anybody else that Robert would go to if the deal required programming."

"Would that have changed with Robert knowing about Chuck's interest in Stephanie?"

"Maybe, but I don't think so, at least not in the early stages. The argument they had over Stephanie didn't happen until recently."

"And you're sure that the alleged affair between the two of them was not the cause of Chuck's death."

"Maybe 'sure' would be too strong a word."

"What word would you use, Angela?"

" 'Confident.' "

"Same thing."

"Okay, let me put it in terms that you understand, Mr. Lawyer." It was obvious that Angela was becoming frustrated with Marcus and his questions. It was getting late and they had been at it for hours. She wanted to stop, tell Marcus to go home, but then she remembered two things. One, that Marcus had no home to go to, and two, she knew that it was her freedom on the line. "I couldn't say beyond a reasonable doubt that Robert killed Chuck over his alleged affair with Stephanie."

"Thank you. Now, Robert said things had changed and he was referring to Chuck. Did he mention that Chuck's death is what changed?"

"Yes, but not until Floyd said that he didn't know what Robert was talking about. Robert said Chuck is dead behind this shit. Excuse my language."

"It's all right, Angela. I've heard you curse before. As I remember you used to curse like a sailor."

"That was a long time ago, Marcus," Angela cooed, and sat down on the couch next to him. "Over the years I've been trying to clean up my act."

"Yes, you're quite the polished professional these days." Marcus thought about kissing her. "What happened after that?"

"By that time both of them were starting to get a little heated, but they were trying to keep their voices down."

"Because there were still people in the office."

"Yes."

"Who was there?"

"The receptionist, Floyd's personal assistant. I really can't say who else. I can only assume that it was Floyd's personal assistant that heard me say, 'Stop it.'"

Marcus looked at Angela without speaking for a moment. "Since I think it's safe to assume that Floyd didn't tell her that he had tried to rape you, I don't ever want you to mention that again. Not to the police, not even to me."

Angela smiled a sly smile. "I thought you didn't want me to leave anything out?"

"I did say that, but that is only when you are talking to me. I will tell you what you should or should not say to the police. Your revelation that Floyd tried to rape you will give Pryor the motive that he's looking for and he will arrest you on the spot."

"I understand." Angela winked at Marcus. "No more rape talk."

"So the argument is getting heated. What did Floyd say when Robert mentioned what happened to Chuck?"

"That's when Floyd said that he had taken steps to ensure that what happened to Chuck would never happen to them. They went back and forth with, you know, 'No, you can't.' 'Yes, I can.' That's when I said, 'Stop it.'"

"What happened then?"

"Everybody took a breath, and then Robert said that I was right, that this wasn't getting them anywhere. That the fact of the matter was that Floyd couldn't guarantee anything. And Floyd said that that was Robert's opinion, and that he knew what he was doing. That Robert just needed to trust him, and that things would work out exactly the way they were planned. Robert said that he couldn't trust Floyd anymore and that he was pulling out. That Floyd could tell his contact that the deal was off."

"How did Floyd take that?"

"He told Robert that would be a mistake. And that he would live to regret it. Robert asked if that was a threat, and Floyd said no, it was a fact. That Robert had no idea of who these people were and what they were capable of."

"What did Robert say to that?"

"He said that he would have to take his chances, and that's when we left," Angela said, and let out a deep yawn.

Marcus looked at his watch and noticed that it was after two thirty. He thought about his stalker, and that she had called him the last couple of nights at two forty-five. "I didn't realize that it was this late."

"I did."

"Why don't we call it a night? We'll pick this up on Monday."

"That's what you said last night, Marcus, and here we are."

"I'm serious this time."

"Did you want to stay here tonight?" Angela asked, and thought for a moment about what might happen between them if he stayed. She quickly pushed the thoughts of riding him out of her mind. Besides, she knew that if she allowed him to stay there they would get right back to it as soon as Marcus opened his eyes, and she was tired of talking about it. The more they talked about it, the more it seemed that Robert had betrayed her trust and left her for the police.

"No, I think I've imposed on you too much already, don't you think?"

"Not at all. Your house was burned to the

ground. That's what friends are for," Angela said, glad that he had taken that choice away from her.

"True, but I think that it would be better if I got a room somewhere. Or maybe I'll take Garrett up on his offer to let me stay at his place."

"Who's Garrett?"

"He's a private investigator that I work with sometimes. He's also a good friend. You'll meet him, I'm sure, as this progresses."

"I'm sure."

At two forty-five Marcus's cell phone rang.

"Hot date?" Angela asked, but Marcus didn't say anything. He looked at the display before answering. The display said UNKNOWN.

Marcus took a deep breath and then pressed TALK. "Hello," he said tentatively.

"Are you having a good time, lover?"

"Who is this?"

"I told you, I'm nothing, I'm nobody."

"What do you want from me?"

"I don't want anything from you, not anymore. I just wanted to tell you that you're gonna need to call a cab or something when you're finished making her come like a maniac."

"What are you talking—" But the stalker ended the call.

"Was that her, your stalker?"

"Yes."

"What did she say?"

Marcus stood up and started for the door. "She said that I was going to need to call a cab," he told Angela, purposely leaving out the part of his making her come like a maniac. He didn't want to alarm her.

"What does that mean?" Angela asked, and followed Marcus to the door.

"I don't know but I think checking on my car would be a good idea. Stay here." Marcus opened the door and went outside.

Angela followed him out the door. "I wanna see."

When Marcus got to the car, he could see that all four tires were flat and that the word LOVER was spray-painted all over the car.

"Shit!" Marcus yelled.

Angela let out a little giggle.

"What's so funny?"

"Nothing, Marcus, I mean, I'm not laughing because of what she did to the car. I was just thinking that you have got to have awesome sexual skills to make a woman do all this to you, that's all." Angela laughed. "Maybe next time you won't lay it down so hard. Some of us girls just can't take it."

"Right. I'll try to remember that."

Chapter 17

It was almost three o'clock in the morning and Robert still hadn't found what he was looking for. He was tired physically and felt mentally drained, but he had to focus. He had to think through this, because he understood what the consequences of failure were. These people had killed for this, so not only was his life at stake, but Angela's life as well.

Feeling that he had no other options available to him and with everything on the line, Robert drove away from Floyd's house, but his mind was still on the night that Floyd was killed.

"That didn't go well at all," Angela had said to him that night after they left Floyd's office. "I'm sorry."

"What are you sorry about?"

"I let things get out of hand, overplayed my part. And I was so close to him telling me everything. I could feel it."

Robert reached over and took Angela's hand into his. Then he kissed it gently. "It's not your fault that no man can resist you. It's my fault. I should never have asked you to do it. Never put you in a position for that to happen. I should have known that with Floyd feeling the way he felt about you, something like this could happen."

"How would you know that Floyd was capable of trying to force himself on me? The answer is that you couldn't."

"Maybe," Robert said, and let go of Angela's hand. "But it was still the wrong thing to do and I'm sorry. I promise that nothing like that will ever happen again. I love you, Angela. You mean everything to me. I wouldn't be able to live with myself if anything ever happened to you because of me."

Robert thought about those words that he had said to her that night, because in spite of his efforts, that's exactly what he had done.

"So what now?" Angela asked that night.

"I'm going to put you in a cab, and then I'm going back to talk to Floyd."

"Are you sure that's the best move at this point?"

"No. But I still need to know exactly what Floyd is up to and who he's in it with. Chuck was murdered because of this."

"And you still think that you can't tell me what this is all about, Robert?"

"Yes."

"Even after all this, you still can't tell me?"

Robert remembered the look of disappointment in her eyes. He wanted to tell her everything, but this wasn't the time. "Angela, the less you know about this, the better it will be for you. Especially now. I hate like hell that I ever got any of you involved in this mess. Now it's up to me to make this right. I think I owe Chuck that much."

Robert took out his cell phone and called a cab for Angela. Then he called Floyd and told him that he still needed to talk to him. "I'm glad you called, Robert. I knew you're too smart to let this opportunity get past you."

"I'm a lot of things Floyd, but stupid isn't one of them. But, Floyd, when I get there, I need you to tell me the truth. No more lies, no more games. There's a lot at stake here. I think that I deserve to know exactly what you've got me involved in."

When he returned to Floyd's office, the only car in the parking lot was Floyd's. Everybody else had gone for the evening. Robert parked his car in the office complex a few blocks away and walked back. Once he was at the building, he went inside and found Floyd seated behind his desk.

"Are you alone this time, Robert?"

"Yes. I put Angela in a cab and sent her home."

"What have you told her?"

"Nothing. How could I tell her anything when I don't really know anything?"

"Would you mind opening your jacket, Robert?"

Robert looked at Floyd strangely and thought about his request. Then it hit him. "I don't have a gun, Floyd." Robert held open both sides of his jacket.

"Thank you, Robert. I know that you're not the type to carry a gun. But after what just happened with Angela, I'm sure you understand my need to be careful in my future dealings with you."

"I understand. After what happened to Chuck, you understand my need to know what's really going on here."

"Have a seat, Robert. Can I get you a drink?" Floyd asked, and Robert accepted. Floyd reached for the bottle of single malt scotch and a couple of glasses that he had on the credenza behind him. "Humor me for a minute," Floyd said as he poured. "Angela was here acting on your instructions, attempting to get information from me, wasn't she?"

"She was."

"You're in love with her, aren't you?"

"I am."

"I thought as much. I could tell by the look in your eyes when you came charging through that door to rescue her." Floyd laughed. "That kind of anger only comes from loving somebody. She's an extraordinary woman. It takes that kind of woman to do what she did for you."

"I know."

"But I'm curious."

"What about?"

"Why did you think you had to go to that extreme to get information? All you had to do was ask me. I would have told you whatever you wanted to know. I just wasn't about to tell you in front of her."

"You never have seemed interested in giving me any details before."

"Chuck dying changed that, Robert. I know you think that I'm a heartless prick and I have no feelings for Chuck and what happened to him. You probably think I had something to do with it, or that I killed him myself."

"The thought had occurred to me," Robert said as he sipped his scotch.

"I assure you that I didn't kill him. I only found out later that he was dead. At that point I knew that they had killed him and that my life was in danger too. Was Chuck acting on your instructions?"

"No. I didn't have anything to do with that. I had no idea what Chuck had in mind," Robert lied. "What happened to Chuck?"

"Chuck called me that day and said he wanted to meet to deliver the enhancement he made to the program. When I got there Chuck gave me the program and said that the files were encrypted and that he wanted to make a side deal with me. He said that you hadn't been honest with him about the money. Chuck said that since he was doing all the work on the program he deserved more money. I told him that my deal was with you and that if he wanted a bigger share he would have to talk to you. He said that was unacceptable. That he didn't want you to know what he was doing, so if I wanted the encryption I would come up with the money."

"What did you say to that?"

"I told him that I would have to talk with my backers and I would get back to him."

"Since you had the program you really didn't need him anymore so you had him killed."

"No. I only found out later that Chuck had followed me when I went to talk to my contact. They didn't know who he was. All they knew was that he was following them, so they killed him."

Robert remembered thinking at that moment, why did Chuck try to follow them? At that point, Chuck knew who they were, and their suspicions had been confirmed. Why put his life on the line any more than he already had by following them? And why did he give Floyd the program, when they both agreed that they couldn't give it to him?

"Where's the program now?"

"It's safe."

"So you haven't given it to your contact?"

"There would be no point in that. The files are encrypted. I've tried everything I know to decrypt them, but I can't do it. I was hoping that you might be some help with that."

"I'm nowhere near the programmer that Chuck was. If he didn't want you in those files you're not getting in." Robert recalled feeling relieved that even though Floyd had the program, he couldn't do anything with it. He felt like Chuck had not died for nothing.

So it was over, but he still had to know what was going on because he still needed to talk to the FBI about Floyd and his terrorist friends, but Floyd had other ideas. When Robert looked up, Floyd was pointing a gun at him.

"What's the gun for, Floyd?"

"I told you what a careful guy I am."

"You want me to put my hands up?"

"I don't think that will be necessary, Robert. Just stand up and keep your hands where I can see them."

Robert complied with his request.

"Now I want you to come over here and decrypt those files."

Robert got up from his chair and walked slowly around the desk with his hands out in front of him where Floyd could see them. As soon as he was close enough he swung quickly and knocked the gun out of Floyd's hand.

Both men went for the gun and after a brief struggle Robert came up with it.

Robert pointed the gun at him. "Get up," he instructed, and Floyd did as he was told.

"You want me to put my hands up?" Floyd asked with a smile on his face.

"I don't think that will be necessary, Floyd. Just sit down and, oh yeah, keep your hands where I can see them."

Floyd sat down and put the palms of his hands on the desk. "What do we do now, Robert?"

"You were going to sell that program to terrorists, weren't you?"

"No, Robert, *we* are selling the program for money. Who *our* contacts are and what they do with the program after they've paid for it is not my concern."

"There is no *we* in this. Those are not *our* contacts. This is all your doing, Floyd. You told me that your company was developing a product to compete in the market. I would never have gotten involved in any of this if you told me what you really intended to do with it."

"What's the difference, Robert? We're being well paid for what we're doing."

"There you go again with this we shit," Robert said, and pushed the gun to Floyd's temple.

"Yes, we! You are as much a part of this now as I am. So what are you going to do now, call the police?"

"The thought had crossed my mind."

"And tell them what? That you were selling your company's trade secrets for millions of dollars? Because that's all you can tell them. You have no idea who my contacts are, all you'll have is me. By the time the police get around to looking for these alleged terrorists you keep mentioning, they will be long gone. Disappeared like the shadows they are."

"We'll see about that."

"Don't be a fool, Robert. Decrypt those files and make this money and disappear. Three million dollars should be enough to ease your conscience."

"No, Floyd, it won't. Chuck is dead. Nothing, especially money, will ever ease my conscience about that. So here's what's going to happen now. You're going to give me that program and then you're going to tell me who these people are and where I can find them."

"Or what? You'll kill me?"

"Don't think I won't."

"You won't kill me, Robert, you're not the type that commits murder in cold blood. But they will kill you, because that's the type of people they are. Now put the gun down and get started on the files."

"I told you what's going to happen here."

"No." Floyd pressed his temple against the barrel of the gun. "Go ahead and kill me. Without the decryption on those files I'm dead already."

"You're not leaving me much choice."

"I know, and since I know that you're not going to kill me the only choice you have is to do what I said and get paid!" Floyd yelled.

"No!" Robert yelled, and pulled the trigger.

Robert wiped his fingerprints off the gun and left the office.

"Now it's over," Robert said aloud as he made his way back to his car.

With the programmer and the middleman dead, Robert was sure that it was over and Floyd's contacts, whoever they were, would disappear. The reality that he was so wrong about everything came crashing down on him when he found out that Stephanie was dead.

The only thing that Robert could think to do was to give them what they wanted and hope that he lived through the exchange. Once he knew who the men were, he could go to the FBI. But he understood what that meant. He would be giving men whom he believed were terrorists information that would compromise American defense capabilities at a time of war. That too was unacceptable, but what choice did he have?

His plan now was simple. Robert drove as fast as he could to his office. Once again, he parked his car a few blocks away and walked back to the building. He used the executive entrance, so he would not have to be bothered with security. He knew that they would find in the morning that he had been there because of the security protocols, but by then he would be long gone with what he came for.

Once he got in the parking garage and the executive entrance, it occurred to Robert that the possibility existed that once his code was entered, security or even the police would be notified. Robert entered Angela's access code and was in.

All he had to do now was make it to his office without being detected. When he reached his office, Robert downloaded the original program that the company had developed and got out of there. He returned to his apartment to make the modifications that Floyd had asked Chuck to make. Then Robert made some minor adjustments so the program would appear to be genuine, but wouldn't work in operation, and hoped that it would be enough.

Chapter 18

Marcus stood outside Angela's house, cursing as he looked at the damages his stalker had done to his car. "Damn it!" Marcus yelled, and kicked the car, as Angela looked on and tried to calm him down.

"Why don't you come back inside so you can call the police, Marcus?" Angela told him as she began noticing the lights of her nosy neighbors coming on. "Standing out here yelling isn't going to do you any good. I mean, it's not like you don't have insurance."

Marcus snapped his head around and looked at Angela with fury in his eyes. "Okay, okay," he said, realizing that she was right, and tried to calm himself down.

Angela took his hand in hers and led him back toward the house. The warmth of her hand seemed to calm him down, but this was short-lived.

When he got to the front door, Marcus stopped in his tracks and looked around the area. In his anger over seeing his car with all four tires flat and the word LOVER spray-painted all over it, he realized that the stalker had followed him to Angela's house and was probably still in the area.

Instead of going inside, Marcus turned and walked back toward the car.

"Where are you going?" Angela asked.

"Go inside and lock the door. I'll be right back."

"Do you want me to call the police?"

"I'll call them when I get back. Right now you need to go back inside and lock the door, Angela," Marcus said as he walked.

When he got to the street, Marcus looked in both directions to see if he saw anybody. It was too dark for him to really see very far. He opened the trunk and got out his flashlight. Marcus held up the light and shone it in both directions down the dimly lit street. Not seeing anything, but sure that they were someplace nearby, watching, Marcus began walking down the street.

As he walked, Marcus replayed in his mind the two conversations he'd had with the stalker, and tried to pick up on something in the way the caller spoke and put a name and a face to it.

You can't hide from me.

Who is this?

You didn't think you could just throw me away and move on to the next one.

What are you talking about? Who is this?

Oh, I'm nothing, I'm nobody. So don't worry, after a while I'll go away and you can go back to your normal life and your new BMW and your big house. Oh yeah, I forgot, you don't have a house to go home to.

What? What do you mean?
Go home and see.

He had gone home to find that his house had been set on fire. After that call, he should have known from the first call that she intended to target his car. Marcus cursed himself for not picking up on that not too subtle hint.

Are you having a good time, lover?
Who is this?
I told you, I'm nothing, I'm nobody.
What do you want from me?
I don't want anything from you, not anymore.

Two things stuck in his mind, the word *lover,* and *not anymore.* He still had it in his mind that it might be Panthea Daniels that was making her presence felt. However, he still had a real problem believing that she was capable of burning his house to the ground and destroying his car. *She might break a nail and she would definitely find that unacceptable.*

The fact that Marcus didn't think she was capable, more than anything else, he felt eliminated her as a suspect. Panthea was far too ladylike to do anything like this. Regardless of how he felt, he was still anxious to know if Garrett had looked into her whereabouts.

After circling the block and finding nothing, Marcus went back to Angela's house to call the police. When he got back, he found Angela sitting on the steps waiting for him to come back.

"Well?" Angela stood up and opened the door to go inside.

Marcus followed her in, closed the door, and locked it behind him. "I didn't find anybody out there."

"Did you really expect to?"

"Not really."

"Mind if I ask you a question?"

"No, go ahead."

"If you did find somebody out there, what were you gonna do, hit them with your flashlight?"

Marcus looked at Angela and a smile crept across his face. "I guess that was kind of stupid."

"For a really smart guy, that was a really stupid move."

"Where's your phone?"

"No need, the police are on their way."

"Thank you," Marcus said, and plopped down on Angela's couch.

"No problem. I figured with you out wandering around looking for her, I should call the police. You know, just in case you caught her or your trusty flashlight didn't get the job done," Angela giggled.

"Okay, Angela. I already admitted how stupid that was. You don't have to beat me over the head with it."

"You mean the way you've been beating me all over my body about some of the stupid things I've been in the last couple of weeks?"

"Touché."

"And what happened to 'I'm sure I wasn't fol-lowed here, Angela, so I think you'll be safe,' huh? What happened to that?"

"Well, if you wanted to be technical about it—"

"And I don't."

"You are still safe. Your car is parked in the driveway. She didn't bother it. And she didn't set the house on fire."

"Whatever, Marcus. I think that had more to do with the fact that we were in here. Whoever this nut is, I don't think she means to kill you. Just make you regret ever knowing her."

"She's done that, believe me. I just want to know for sure who she is, and put a stop to this madness before it goes any further."

"A friend of mine had a stalker. That woman was a mess. But she wasn't his girlfriend or anything like that. Just a one-night stand he picked up at the club. After that she developed this delusional belief that he was in love with her and that they were meant to be together. She used to write him letters and poems detailing their psychic connection to each other. No matter what he said, or how he denied it, she knew the truth."

"I'm not sure I wanna hear this."

"He tried everything to get away from her. He even moved to Chicago to get away from her."

"Did it work?"

"No. She tracked down where he lived through a detective agency that gave her his new address, what kind of car he drove, who he called, and where he worked."

"How'd it end?"

"Honestly, I don't know. The last time I called

him the number was disconnected. I never heard from him again."

"These things usually end one of two ways. The stalker usually moves on to stalk somebody else, or it ends violently."

"Since your stalker has already escalated to violence, I guess you know where this is going."

"That's why I need to find out who it is and put a stop to it before it goes any further."

While Marcus waited for the police to get there, he called Garrett, explained what had happened, and told him what the stalker said and asked him to pick him up. After he got through getting his laugh on about it, Garrett said he would be there as soon as he could.

When the police arrived, they took statements from Marcus and Angela. Since she wasn't romantically involved with Marcus, Angela didn't know why she had to give a statement. The officer explained that it was just procedure, but Angela knew better. She knew that since the stalker had followed him to her house, and since the stalker said that she had moved on to the next one, the stalker might think that she was the next one.

Shortly after the police left and Marcus's car was towed away, Garrett arrived at Angela's house. He found Marcus waiting outside.

"What's up, lover boy? Was that your car I just saw going down the street?" Garrett laughed.

"Don't start, Garrett, I'm just not in the mood."

"I'm sorry, big dawg. But you gotta admit, if it

was happening to somebody else, this shit would be funny as hell."

"Yeah, but since it is me, that shit ain't funny at all," Marcus said with a grin on his face.

"Then why you got that shit-eatin' grin plastered on your face?"

"Because if it was happening to somebody else, it would be funny. You saw the car, Garrett, she fucked it up. But what ain't funny is that now I have no home, no car, and all I have left are the clothes on my back."

"You're right, that ain't funny worth a damn. I'm sorry."

"Don't sweat it, let's just get out of here," Marcus said, and started walking toward Garrett's car, but Garrett didn't move from where he was standing. "What?" Marcus asked, stopping.

"You ain't gonna introduce me to the lovely Ms. Pettybone? From what I hear, it's a show that you don't wanna miss."

"She's gone to sleep. That's why I was waiting outside. You'll meet Angela soon enough. So can we go now?"

Once they were in Garrett's car and away from Angela's house, he noticed that Marcus kept looking behind them. "What are you doing?"

"Checking to see if somebody is following us," Marcus advised, and kept looking out the back window. "She obviously followed me to Angela's. I wouldn't be surprised if she was following us now."

"That's not a problem. If she's back there let's see what kind of skills she got," Garrett said, and stepped on the gas. "She got to be one hell of a driver if she's going to keep up with us now."

"Stay on surface streets, keep away from the interstate."

"Good idea. She may be waiting somewhere close to the interstate, waiting for us to pass. But while you're looking behind you, remember, the best tail is from the front."

"Why is that?"

"Because you're looking behind you. I stay in front of you, watching you in my rearview."

"What happens when I turn?"

"I turn at my first opportunity and canvass the area until I find where you went or reacquire you."

"I guess that makes sense." Marcus relaxed in his seat. "What have you found out?"

"In your current state of mind I'm guessin' that you wanna know what Mrs. Daniels is up to."

"Good guess. Did you talk to her?"

"Nope."

"Why not?"

"Currently, Panthea Daniels is on day five of a ten-day cruise. Right now she should be in Barbados. It took a little doing, but I was able to confirm with the cruise line that she did board the ship."

"I don't know if that makes me feel better or worse."

"It makes you feel better, and you know it. You really didn't wanna believe that it was her anyway. I know you had real feelings for her."

If he was going to be honest with himself and this was one of those times, Marcus had to admit that

Garrett was right. As much as he wanted to classify her as a mistake in judgment in getting involved with a client, he loved Panthea, loved everything about her. "Let's start exploring other possibilities."

"Like what?"

"Like maybe it's some mad-crazy ex-client, fresh out of prison, who spent years thinking about how he or she was going to terrorize, then torture me to death."

"You have a point."

"I'm glad that you see that. Especially since you told me."

"I'm on it."

"So, what else have you got?"

"I checked with Dekalb police. They weren't able to find any fingerprints at your house when they checked it. Obviously I'm talkin' 'bout before she burned it to the ground."

"Obviously."

"I checked with the arson investigator. He said he hasn't finished his investigation yet, but he doubts if there will be anything that will provide any leads. So it's all on us. We're going to need to come up with a suspect."

"You think Angela will be all right?"

"Hard to say. Her anger seems directed at you, not Angela. She knows where she lives, was there long enough to fuck up your shit. If she wanted to fuck with Angela, she'd have fucked up her car too."

"That was my thinking too."

"But if you want, I could free up some time and,

you know, extend my personal protection to the lovely Ms. Pettybone."

"You'd like that, wouldn't you?"

"If she's all y'all keep tellin' me she is, then yes."

"I don't think that's necessary, but if you have an operative free, it wouldn't hurt if they checked on her."

"I'll make that happen, but tell me something?"

"What's that?"

"What were you doing there at damn near three o'clock in the morning?"

"Talking about her case," Marcus told him, although there were times that he wished it was for other reasons.

"Right."

"Seriously, we were talking about her case."

"And I'm not sayin' that you weren't, but I'm not the one stalking you."

"I see your point, she'll think it was more than just talk going on."

"I mean, most lawyers consult with their clients during regular business hours, not at damn near three o'clock in the morning. But what I really wanna know is, a woman breaks into your house, more than once. Trashes your bedroom, takes a knife to your bed, and then burns it to the ground. Why did you think it was a good idea to go spend your Saturday night with the lovely Ms. Pettybone?"

Marcus looked at Garrett without answering.

"I'm just askin'."

"Okay, it was a stupid move on my part."

"As long as you know, I won't bring it up again."

"I know this is your weekend with the kids, but what else did you find out?"

"Not much, it is the weekend, you know."

"When has that ever stopped you?"

"What can I say? It happens. Maybe I'm just getting old and slow," Garrett said as he pulled up in front of his apartment building.

"Well, you enjoy the rest of your weekend with your family," Marcus said, and started to get out of the car.

"One more thing before you go. Stay away from the lovely Ms. Pettybone for a while until this stalker is caught. For her sake."

"Yes, Daddy."

"I'm serious, Marcus. I know once you get goin' on something you don't let up. For whatever reason, maybe because she's an old friend who is fine as hell." Garrett paused and looked at Marcus. "At least that's what I'm told."

Marcus gave Garrett a look, but he knew it was both. Angela was an old friend and she was fine as hell. Even if he never got the chance to touch her, being in Angela's presence, and admiring her beauty was a good thing.

"You're on this one hard."

"It's because she's an old friend. Nothing more."

"And I'm not sayin' that it ain't. All I'm sayin' is, think with the big head, and stay away from her."

"I promise that I won't go back to Angela's house anymore this weekend."

"And one more thing."

Chapter 19

"What's that?" Marcus asked.

"Take this," Garrett said, and took out his gun.

"No, thank you, Garrett. You know how I feel about guns. I barely look at the one I have, or I could say had."

"And you know how I feel about friends of mine gettin' dead."

"I really don't think that's necessary, Garrett. I'll be all right without that."

"Maybe you will. But it's better to be safe than dead." Marcus didn't say anything. "Look, I know how you feel about guns, and I respect that. But what you don't know is who is stalkin' you and how far they are willing to take this. You're already homeless and you don't have a car, the next step is—"

"You made your point," Marcus said reluctantly.

"Good. Now take this gun and go get you some sleep, you look like shit."

"I haven't been sleeping well lately," Marcus said, and took the gun from Garrett.

"Betsy there will help you sleep better. And turn off your cell phone. Better yet, give it to me. If she calls, I'll talk to her. See if I can't keep her talking long enough to trace the call. If I find out anything I'll call you on the house phone. If you leave the house before I get back, call me. And stay away from Angela."

"Thanks, Garrett."

"For what?"

"Everything," Marcus said, and got out of the car.

After watching Garrett drive off, Marcus went inside Garrett's apartment and locked the door behind him. He stretched out on the couch and put the gun on the coffee table. He thought about Angela and it wasn't long before he was fast asleep.

A few hours later, Garrett was in his son Gary's room, shaking him. "Get up and get dressed. We gotta make a run."

Gary covered his head with the pillow. "Why I gotta go?"

"'Cause I said so. Now get up and get dressed. Come on down when you're ready," Garrett said, and walked out of the room.

When Gary had come down the steps, Garrett got up and walked out the door. They had been driving for a while when Gary finally asked the only question on his mind. "Where are we going?"

"We're going to see Mr. Douglas."

"Cool."

"I'm glad that you approve," Garrett replied, and kept driving.

As they drove a little farther, Gary noticed that they weren't going in the direction of Marcus's house. "You mind if I ask you a question?"

"What's that?"

"If we're going to see Mr. Douglas, why are we going to your place?"

"You ask a lot of questions."

"You the one that taught me to question everything."

"You do pay attention to what I say," Garrett said, and a part of him felt some sense of pride.

Maybe he had gotten through to his son on some level.

"You do be right sometimes. Sometimes."

"What kind of English is that?"

When Gary shrugged his shoulders, Garrett simply shook his head.

"You still haven't answered my question," Gary said as they parked in front of Garrett's apartment. "Why are we here if we're going to see Mr. D?"

"'Cause he's inside," Garrett said, and got out of the car.

Gary hurried to keep up with him. "What Mr. D doing in there? And where is his car?" he asked.

"'Cause Mr. Douglas doesn't have a home or a car anymore."

Garrett unlocked the door and the Mason men went inside. They found Marcus fast asleep with the gun on the coffee table. Once Garrett felt comfortable that Marcus was all right, he and Gary left the apartment. Once they were in the car, Gary asked the question.

"Why is Mr. D sleeping on your couch and why he got a gun sitting there?"

"He's having some problems and he needed a place to stay, that's all."

"Cool. What is it? Like are gangsters trying to kill him and he's using your crib as a safe house?"

Garrett laughed. "Something like that."

"Come on, Dad, give it up."

"Mr. Douglas has a stalker."

"Cool."

"Boy, you got strange ideas about what's cool. This woman set his house on fire and wrecked his car."

"Oh," Gary said, and felt stupid. "That shit ain't cool at all."

"I'm glad you see it that way. And watch your mouth."

"Sorry. But I do know right from wrong. I know that people should have respect for other people's privacy and their property."

"Damn, you do pay attention when I talk to you."

"Like I said, you do be right sometimes."

When Marcus opened his eyes later that afternoon, he was very surprised to find Garrett's youngest daughter, Monique, and Gary watching television.

"Hi, Mr. Douglas," Monique said to him.

"Hi," Marcus said, and tried to clear his head.

"Hey, Dad, he's awake," Gary called to his father, who was in the bedroom. "What's up, Mr. D?"

"Not exactly running out in front today."

Garrett came into the room. "I thought I told you two not to bother Mr. Douglas."

"We didn't, Daddy, he just woke up," Monique said to her father.

"You think the TV had something to do with that?" Garrett scolded.

"It's okay, Garrett." Marcus sat up and rubbed his palms over his face. "What time is it anyway?" he asked even though he had on a watch.

"Three forty-five," Gary announced.

"I've been out for a while."

"You needed the rest. I came to tell you that I had Janise reserve you a car. It's waiting for you at the airport. If you want, we could roll by the mall and you can get some clothes on the way to pick it up."

"You told Janise?"

"She saw the fire on the news, and called me."

"The news? I didn't see any news crews at the house when I got there."

"It was on today at noon. She said they didn't have pictures of the actual fire. They just showed a file photo, and footage of you at the Ferguson trial, and a shot of the ashes that used to be your house."

"Great."

"You are kind of a celebrity in this town. But wait, it gets better. The reporter said that there are uncon-firmed reports that your car was recently vandal-ized. You, naturally, were unavailable for comment," Garrett said, and held up Marcus's cell phone.

"They called?"

"Yes. I told them that I couldn't confirm or deny any incidents of vandalism. And that you were unavailable for comment."

"So you're my press secretary now?"

"Ha, ha, Daddy's a secretary," Monique mused, and Garrett gave her a look.

"Come on, Monique. Let's watch TV in Dad's room," Gary told his sister, and started for the room.

"But that TV is so small I can barely see it," Monique said, and got up.

"Tell your mama to buy me a bigger one for Christmas," Garrett said, and his children went into the bedroom.

Once they were gone, Marcus turned to Garrett. "You think whoever's doing this called the press?"

"I'm sure of it. Probably right after I talked to her."

"Then she did call?"

"About seven thirty this morning. I called to tell you, and when you didn't answer the phone, I came to check on you."

"I was dead to the world."

"Poor choice of words, but yeah, you were out for the count."

"You've been here that long?"

"We've been in and out, had some errands to run, but we've been checking on you. I don't think she knows about this place or she'd have come by here. You should be safe here for the time being."

"I'm almost afraid to ask what makes you say that."

"She was pretty pissed when she realized it

wasn't you answering the phone. Called me all kinds of mothafuckas and hung up the phone."

"So it wasn't long enough to trace the call?"

"Not even close."

After Marcus took a much-needed shower, he, Garrett, and the kids went to Stonecrest Mall in Lithonia so Marcus could get something to wear. Then it was on to the airport to pick up the car Janise had reserved for him. Once Marcus had the car, a 2007 white Volvo S80 sedan, Garrett followed him back to his apartment.

Once again, Garrett made Marcus promise to stay put and away from Angela, but Marcus had other ideas. As soon as Garrett was gone, he picked up the phone and called Angela.

"Angela, it's Marcus."

"I didn't recognize the number, so I started not to answer."

"I'm at Garrett's apartment."

"How are you?"

"I'm fine."

"Good, I was worried about you. Did you get any rest?"

"Yes, I crashed and I mean crashed hard on his couch."

"You haven't heard any more from your stalker, have you?"

"No. I gave Garrett my cell phone, but I did make the news."

"I know, I saw it. The pictures they have of you don't do you justice. You're much better looking in person."

"You think so?"

"I should know. I've been looking at that face for the last three days."

"Care to go for four?"

"Yes and no."

"What's that supposed to mean?"

"It means yes, I do want to see you," Angela said.

Spending the last few days alone with Marcus had caused her to do a lot of thinking. Thinking about the feeling she had for him, but denied to herself. Thinking about how physically attracted to him that she was both then and now. Thinking about the choices she'd made in her life. Thinking about giving in to her passions. "But no, I don't think it's a good idea," she said, resigned to follow her better judgment. "And I definitely don't want you to come here. I don't want her coming back here again. There's no telling what she might do this time."

"I understand," Marcus said, obviously disappointed, but he understood her reasoning, though unwilling to give up that easily. "I don't have to come over there. You could come over here," he offered, but then he thought about it. Garrett and the kids might come back. "Or we could meet someplace for dinner."

"I don't know, Marcus."

"Have you had dinner yet?"

"No, and I'm hungry."

"Then it's settled. Where do you wanna meet?"

Angela thought for a minute. "I need to go by my office to pick up some things. I decided that

I'm not going in tomorrow. Why don't you meet me there in an hour and a half?"

"Okay, I'll be there at nine."

After hanging up the phone with Marcus, Angela got up and began to get ready to meet him. She wanted to look nice for him, but didn't want to wear anything provocative or too dressy. She settled for an Evan-Picone-Matte crepe dress that tied in the back.

When Angela got to the office building, she went to the executive entrance and put in her access code. She was surprised when the system advised her that she had last entered the building at 2:47 that morning. Since she knew where she was at that time that morning, Angela knew that it had to be Robert.

She immediately took out her cell, but then Angela thought about it. *If he hasn't answered any of your calls, what makes you think that he'll answer now?* Angela put her phone away and went inside to get what she had come for. On the way to her office, Angela thought that he might not answer the phone, but she had a good idea where he might be. Nobody but the two of them knew about the loft. *Our secret hideaway.* Even though he hadn't answered the phone, Robert might be there, and if he was Angela had a few things that she had to say to him.

There was still a part of her that didn't believe that Robert had killed Stephanie and Floyd and left her to take the blame for it, but it had been four days since she had last heard from him. *What else could it be?*

After picking up the papers she intended to work on, Angela went back down in the elevator to wait for Marcus. Once he arrived they would go by the loft to look for Robert.

When Marcus arrived at the building, Angela told him about the access code, and about the loft.

"Something else you forgot to mention."

"Hey, go easy on me. I'm new at this stuff. I don't know what's important from what's not."

"Everything means everything, but I think it's a good idea for us to check it out."

Marcus briefly considered calling Garrett and asking him to meet them there, but he quickly dismissed the idea and went to his car. He followed Angela to the loft, and the two went inside the building. When they got to the door, Angela turned and faced Marcus.

"I think I should go in by myself."

"No, I don't think so. If he's in there, there's no telling what he'll do."

"He won't hurt me, if that's what you're thinking."

"Yes, that's exactly what I'm thinking," Marcus replied, and wished he hadn't left the gun at Garrett's.

"It will be all right," Angela assured him, and unlocked the door.

"Okay, but leave the door open and yell if you need me."

"I will, I promise you that."

Angela went inside the loft alone and left Marcus

wondering if he had done the right thing. After looking around and not finding Robert, Angela went back to the door to get Marcus.

"Well?"

"Robert's not here, but I can tell that he's been here recently. At least he has since the last time I was here."

"When was the last time you were here?"

"Wednesday evening."

"Okay, let's search the place. We're looking for anything that might tell us what he was up to or where he is."

"I understand," Angela said, and the two went about searching.

It wasn't long before Angela was seated at Robert's desk. She searched all the drawers and didn't find anything she felt was useful, but what did she know? Angela wondered, if a clue was staring her in the face, would she recognize it? If nothing else she knew that she could ask Marcus to retrace her search to make sure that she hadn't missed something important. Then Angela's hand bumped into the mouse on the desk and Robert's computer screen sprang to life.

Angela looked at the images on the screen, and didn't like what she saw. She quickly clicked on one of the other tabs and found the code Robert had been working on. Angela wasn't much of a programmer, but she knew enough to know that the images were of missiles and code for the contract Integrated had worked on for the Defense Department.

"Marcus!"

"What?"

"I think I found something."

"Where are you?"

"In the office."

"That tells me a lot," Marcus said, and followed the sound of her voice.

"Second door on the left," Angela said, and when she looked up from the screen, Marcus was standing behind her.

"What you got?"

"I'm not one hundred percent sure, but this looks like the code for the missile guidance system that we developed for the DOD."

"So he was doing some work."

"Robert doesn't do much programming anymore and besides, we delivered the finished product months ago."

"I see. So the question is, what is he doing looking at it now? Didn't you say that Floyd's company was bidding on the contract and that's how they met?"

"Yes." Angela looked at Marcus and a look of horror washed across her face.

"What?"

"I think that Robert was trying to sell the program to Floyd."

"It fits. That would explain Floyd. For one reason or another, things went wrong or got away from Robert and he could have killed Floyd for it."

"I think so," Angela said quickly, and admitted to herself for the first time that Robert might actually have killed Floyd.

"What that doesn't explain is Stephanie Covey and Chuck Prentice. If this is what Floyd was killed over, how does it involve them?"

"I told you, Chuck was the best programmer in the company. And he was the lead on this project. If there were any changes to be made to the program, Robert would have to go to him."

"Because he doesn't do much programming. But would he trust Chuck with something like that?"

"They were close friends, at least before Stephanie, that is."

"Okay, tie it to Stephanie?" Marcus asked, feeling that it was important for Angela to put the pieces together for herself.

"Chuck told Stephanie and he had to kill her too."

"It's thin, but at least it gives us a place to start. It's more than we had before we came here."

Chapter 20

While Marcus and Angela tried to put together what they thought were the pieces of the puzzle, Robert waited for Floyd's contact to arrive.

He wanted to meet in a public place, someplace where people would see them, but Floyd's contact would have none of that. He insisted that they meet in the parking lot across from Turner Field. "Park your car at the Comfort Inn on Pollard Boulevard and walk to the lot on the other side of Hank Aaron Drive. Be there at ten. And, Mr. Covey, please come alone."

Since baseball season was over, there was little chance of anybody in that area paying them any attention.

Realizing that going there alone was a bad idea, but feeling that he had little choice in the matter, Robert decided to take some precautions to protect himself in case things got away from him. He realized that as long as he had the program that they wanted, he was safe, but once he handed it over to them they would have no further use for him. Once he finished making the changes to the guidance system that would make the program inoperable, he got back in his car and drove to Tucker, another of the many Atlanta suburbs. Once Robert got where he was going, he made a call. "Kiel, it's Robert."

"Man, what the fuck have you gotten yourself involved in?"

"It's a long story."

"I can't even imagine. When the police left me a message to call them about you, I didn't know what was going on."

"Did you call them?"

"Of course I did."

"What did they say?"

"They just wanted to know if I'd seen you. I told them we were fishing for the last couple of days. They wanted to know where we were, who saw us there."

"I hope you told them want they wanted to know?"

"Why wouldn't I?"

Feeling Kiel's ability to verify that he was out of town while Stephanie was murdered, Robert relaxed a bit. "Just wanted to make sure."

"What the fuck is going on?"

"Stephanie is dead."

"What?"

"Murdered."

"They think you did it?"

"That's what Anthony told me when I got back."

"Well, you were with me and plenty of people saw us there, so at least you have an alibi. But, man, I'm sorry about Stephanie. If there's anything I can do for you, just ask."

"There is something you can do for me."

"Anything, man, just ask and it's done."

"Come outside."

"Say again."

"I'm parked outside, Kiel. Come on out."

"Oh."

It didn't take long before Kiel was out the door and on his way to Robert's car. Robert got out of his car to greet Kiel. "I don't have a lot of time, so I don't have time to explain, but I need a really big favor."

"Anything."

"I need a gun."

"You, a gun? What for?"

"I told you, Kiel, I don't have time to explain. Can you help me or not?"

"If you want one of my guns, you better make the time. Who you planning on killing?"

As quickly as he could, Robert explained what was going on, without going into any detail. That the people responsible for Stephanie's death wanted something from him and he was going to meet them and needed the gun for protection.

"I'll get a couple of guns and I'll go with you."

"No. They said come alone."

"So?"

"Kiel, three people are already dead because of me. I can't involve anybody else and take the chance that the same thing will happen to you."

Kiel shook his head. "Wait here." He went back

into his house and returned shortly with a small cloth bag.

"Beretta nine millimeter semiautomatic. Fires fifteen from the clip. One is already in the chamber and the safety's off, so all you gotta do is point and squeeze the trigger. I put two extra clips in there, just in case you need them, and a pair of gloves. Serial number is filed off, so it can't be traced back to either of us," Kiel said, and handed Robert the bag.

"Where'd you get this?"

"Don't ask. If you use it, toss it. Neither one of us ever needs to see that gun again after that."

"I understand." Robert turned to get in his car. But he turned back quickly. "Kiel."

"Yeah."

"Thanks."

"I hope you don't need to use that."

"Yeah, me too."

"Good luck. Call me when you can."

"I will," Robert said, and got in his car and drove away.

It was just before ten when Robert parked at the Comfort Inn. He turned off the car, took a deep breath, and thought about what he was about to do.

Thought about dying.

Robert reached for the bag Kiel had given him and took out the gloves. His palms were sweating when he put the gloves on. He tried to think about all the variables. All the things that could happen, all the things that could go wrong. Most of all he thought about how he was going to stay alive. Robert put the program in an old briefcase and got out of the car.

His heart was pounding as he walked toward the stadium to get to the parking lot where the meeting was to take place. Robert was scared and he knew he should be. Nowhere in his wildest imagination could he have come up with a situation like the one he was walking into. *I am no James Bond.* No, he was just the kind of guy who saw a chance to make big money.

The thought of dying that night flashed through his mind again and he tried to block it out. Robert knew he had to stay alive. He knew that altering the program so it wouldn't work wasn't going to be enough. He had to report what he'd done and what he knew. That meant he was going to have to do some time. To a point, Robert thought he deserved it.

When Robert came into the parking lot he saw two men standing by a late-model Lincoln MKZ, which was parked near the back of the lot. As he got closer one of the men began walking in his direction. When the man stopped walking about ten yards away, Robert did too.

"Mr. Covey?"

"Yeah," Robert said, and took a few steps closer.

"Come closer, Mr. Covey. You have nothing more to fear from us. We are businessmen, not American gangsters, bang, bang." The man joked, but Robert didn't laugh. "Did you bring my package?" the man said.

Roy Glenn

"I have it." Robert held up the briefcase. "Do you have the money?"

"I have the money. Bring me the package."

"Money first."

The man waved his hand and the other man came with a metal briefcase. When he reached his partner he stopped to open the case and showed Robert that there was money in it. Since he had no idea what Floyd's deal was for, all he could do was nod his head.

"Put the case down and both of you back away from it," Robert demanded.

"No. You must bring me the package so I can verify that the contents are genuine. Make sure that there are no clever encryptions, like the one your friend added. You could spend that time counting your money."

That was exactly what Robert didn't want to hear. He wanted to drop the program, grab the money, and get away from there. Them wanting to check the program wasn't part of his plan. What if they discovered what he had done?

"Come to the car, let us conclude our business."

"How do I know you won't kill me as soon as I hand you this case?"

"You are most certainly armed. How do I know you won't kill me?"

"What about him?"

"Put the case down and walk away," the man said to his partner. He put the case down and backed away slowly. "That's far enough," the man said without taking his eyes off Robert. "Now, Mr.

Covey, as a show of my good faith, I will walk to the car. Once you have the money, you will join me at the car."

Robert did as the man requested, picked up the money and joined the man at the car. Robert looked at the case; it was filled with stacks of one-hundred-dollar bills, wrapped in ten-thousand-dollar bands. Robert closed the case quickly.

"Aren't you going to count it, Mr. Covey?"

"I'm sure it's all there," he said, preferring instead to keep his attention on staying alive. He put his hand where he could reach the gun easily. "Remember, you're a businessman, not a gangster. Bang, bang."

The man laughed. "The contents appear to be genuine. You are free to go. It was a pleasure doing business with you."

"Right," Robert said, picked up the case, and backed away. When he thought he was far enough away he turned around and started running. At first he heard footsteps coming behind him; then he heard the shot.

The shot startled Robert and he took out his gun and started shooting as he ran. While he was running Robert tripped on a crack in the pavement and dropped the case. He stumbled and hit his head on the ground when he fell. Robert knew he was about to die.

Robert lay there stunned, but he didn't hear anything. Then he heard a car start and drive away quickly. After struggling to his feet, Robert picked up the gun and looked around. "At least they didn't take the money." When he leaned forward to pick up the case he saw the body. One of his wild shots must have hit the man.

Robert thought about waiting for the police and explaining the whole situation. He could give a description of the man, and the kind of car he was driving. He picked up the case and started walking away, quickly dismissing that thought. He dropped his head and looked away when he passed by people walking on the street. By the time he reached his car, he could hear the sirens in the distance. Robert got in his car and drove away slowly, and thought about what he was going to do next.

Chapter 21

Marcus looked over at Angela and noticed that there was a tear rolling down her cheek. "You okay?"

"I thought I knew him."

"We really don't know anybody, just what they show us. Sometimes the truth is ugly."

"Sometimes it's right there and we don't want to see it." Angela stared at the screen and thought back to something Marcus had said. *I guess that explains why you are so willing to protect Robert.* She had told Marcus, *I love him. So whether I trust him or not, whether he killed Floyd and Stephanie, I still love him.*

For Angela, all the pieces began to fall into place. Until now she couldn't see any logical reason for Robert to kill Floyd or Stephanie; therefore, there must be some other explanation. Somebody else who killed them.

"How could I have been so blind not to see this? When all the signs were staring me in the face."

"You mean all the things you thought about but didn't tell me?"

"Yeah, that stuff." Angela laughed a little and Marcus wiped away her tear. "I knew something was going on, that whatever him and Chuck were involved in with Floyd was wrong. But I went along blindly and didn't ask questions when I know I should have." Angela turned to Marcus. "I am so involved in this, at every step. I was Robert's liaison between him and Floyd. I was the one who delivered his messages and who knows what was in all those packages that Robert insisted that I had to take to him. And Chuck, all the interaction I had with him. All the requests Chuck made that I pushed through, never wanting to believe that it would come to all this."

"You knew, didn't you?"

"I guess I did, without actually knowing the details, but all I could see was the pretty picture Robert painted of how wonderful things would be for us when it was over. And that was always followed by 'I just need you to do one more thing.'"

"We need to get out of here, Angela."

"Okay, just give me a minute."

"Sure."

Angela got up and went into the bathroom. She closed the door, leaned against it, and tried to pull herself together. It didn't take long before the load became too much to bear; she broke down and began to cry. Feelings of betrayal consumed her. Betrayal by Robert, whom she loved and who she thought loved her. Angela felt angry with herself for not seeing this coming.

While Angela was in the bathroom, Marcus went into the living room to wait for her. He didn't know if a crime had been committed there or not. Just to be on the safe side, he wiped down everything that he thought he had touched. Just then, Marcus heard what sounded like footsteps coming toward the door. Then he heard keys hit the lock.

The door swung open and Robert Covey walked in carrying the metal briefcase. Robert was caught off guard when he saw Marcus standing there. He pulled out his gun and pointed it at him. "Who are you?"

Marcus held up his hands. "Robert?" Marcus paused. "Don't shoot. My name is Marcus Douglas and I'm a friend of Angela's."

"Angela? Where is she? Angela! Angela!" Robert yelled.

Angela came running out of the bathroom, but stopped when she saw the gun in Robert's hand.

"Who is this, Angela?"

"His name is Marcus Douglas, he's my lawyer."

"Lawyer?" Robert had heard of him, as had most people, from the Ferguson trial. He had also heard Angela talk about Marcus, knew they were friends while they were in college. "What did you tell him?" Robert asked, and took a step closer to Marcus.

Angela didn't say anything, she just stood there frozen at the sight of Robert pointing a gun at Marcus.

"What did you tell him, Angela?" Robert

demanded to know. When Angela didn't answer again, Robert hit Marcus in the head with the butt of his gun and Marcus fell to the floor. Robert stood over Marcus and pointed the gun at him.

"Please, Robert, don't kill him."

Robert tried to calm himself before he spoke. "I'm not going to kill him, Angela. I just need to know what you told him," he said softly.

"He knows everything,"

Robert lowered his gun and came toward Angela. She flinched when he reached out to touch her, and once again the tears began to flow. Robert went into the kitchen and disconnected the cord from the phone. Then he took the cord and tied Marcus's hands and feet. When he was finished Robert picked up the gun and turned to Angela. "I'm not going to hurt you, baby, I promise. Just tell me what you told him."

"He—he—knows that you were trying to sell the program for the missile defense Integrated developed for the government," Angela said through her tears. When Robert heard that he put the gun down. "He knows you killed Stephanie. And you killed Chuck, and Floyd, and you left me to take the blame for it. How could you do that to me? I loved you," Angela said quickly as her pain turned to anger.

"Slow down, Angela. I didn't kill Stephanie. You have got to believe that. I didn't kill Chuck and I had nothing to do with Stephanie's death, Angela. Please, baby, you have got to believe me."

Marcus began to move and Angela knelt down to see about him. The left side of his head was cut and bleeding from the blow he took, and he had a bump on the right side of his head where his head hit the floor. "Are you all right, Marcus?"

He nodded his head and Angela helped him to sit upright against the couch. Once she made Marcus comfortable, Angela turned to Robert. "But you did kill Floyd, didn't you?"

Robert sat down and rested his head in the palms of his hands. "Yes."

"And you set me up to take the blame. How could you do that to me?"

"What are you talking about?"

"What she's talking about is that the police are close to arresting her for Floyd's murder," Marcus managed to say.

"Shut up!" Robert yelled at Marcus. "Nobody asked you to talk."

"You gonna kill me too, Robert?"

"I said shut up!"

"Or what?" Marcus said bravely. "You'll kill me like you did the others?"

"I didn't kill Stephanie or Chuck." Robert dropped his head again. "But I'm the reason they're both dead."

"Listen to me, Robert," Marcus began. "You say you didn't kill Stephanie or Chuck."

"I didn't."

"I believe you, but you need to tell me exactly what happened. Maybe we can sort this whole thing out."

"You don't know anything, do you?"

"No, I really don't. All I've done is speculate

on what happened in an attempt to figure out how
I was going to keep Angela from going to jail for
murders that you committed."

"I told you I didn't kill Stephanie or Chuck, and
I don't have to convince you of anything!" Robert
shouted.

"Why'd you come back?" Angela asked.

"I came back for you, baby. I do love you, I can
make this right, but I need you with me. So please,
Angela, let's go."

"I'm not going anywhere with you until you tell
me what is going on," Angela insisted.

"Angela's right, Robert. If she leaves with you,
then she'll be just as toxic as you are right now.
The police and the FBI are looking for you. Is that
what you want for Angela?"

"I can make this right."

"How, Robert?" Angela came and sat next to
Robert. "How are you going to make this right?
Three people are dead. You said they were dead because of you. I need for you to tell me what is
going on. Please, Robert, if I ever meant anything
to you, you have to tell me what you've gotten me
involved in."

Robert looked at Angela and then to Marcus.
The only way to make things right was to tell the
police and the FBI. To that end, talking to a high-
profile lawyer like Marcus made sense.

"Floyd was trying to sell the program to terrorists.
When Chuck got suspicious I had him follow Floyd.
He saw Floyd meeting with two men and they killed
him for it."

"Oh my God," Angela said.

"After Chuck was murdered and I found out what Floyd was really up to, I knew I couldn't let it go any further."

"So you shot him," Marcus said flatly.

Robert nodded his head. "I thought that would finish it. No Floyd, no deal."

"What about Stephanie? Was she involved in the deal too?" Angela had to know.

"No. As far as I know, Stephanie knew nothing about it. The same people that killed Chuck killed Stephanie."

"Why?" Marcus demanded to know. "If she knew nothing about it, why would they kill her?"

"To get me to cooperate and give them what they wanted. They had already killed Chuck, I couldn't bear the idea that anything would happen to you, Angela."

"Me?"

"They knew about this place. It wouldn't take much for them to find out that your name was on the lease. If I didn't cooperate they might have come after you next."

"So are you saying that you gave it to them?" Angela asked.

"I met them tonight and gave them a program that won't work. One of the men is dead, but the other got away. When he finds out it doesn't work they'll be coming for us. That's why we have got to get out of here, Angela."

"That's why you got to go to the FBI, Robert. It's the only way out of this," Marcus advised.

"I know. But I have got to make sure that Angela is safe. Don't you understand that!"

"The only thing I understand is that if she goes anywhere with you, you'll take her down right along with you. At this point, Angela's involvement is minimal."

"Minimal?" Angela questioned. "I didn't know anything about any of this."

"Do you really want her to suffer for what you did?"

"She won't have to suffer. She'll be safe with me. I've got the money. We can go somewhere. Once we're safe, I'll tell the FBI what I know."

Angela stood up. Robert stood up and started for the door. "I can't go with you, Robert." She turned away.

"Angela, please."

"No, Robert, Marcus is right. The best thing is for you to go to the FBI. I don't want to live my life on the run from the FBI. Not even for you," Angela said without looking in his direction.

Robert picked up the briefcase and started to walk toward the door. Deep inside, he knew that they were both right. All he would be doing is guaranteeing that Angela went down right along with him. "I'm sorry, Angela," he said, and opened the door to leave.

Robert's eyes opened wide as he saw the gun pointed at him. "What—" was all he could get out before he was shot.

Angela heard the shot and turned around in time to see Robert grab his chest and fall to the floor.

She ran to him, knelt down at his side, and took him in her arms. She looked out the open door, but didn't see anybody. "Robert, oh my God, Robert."

"I'm sorry, Angela," Robert said, and died.

"Close the door, Angela," Marcus said, but Angela didn't hear him. She gently closed Robert's eyes and laid his body on the floor. As tears rolled down her cheeks, Angela kissed Robert for the last time.

"Angela!" Marcus shouted, and it got her attention. "Close the door."

"Huh?" she said, still in a daze. "The door, right."

Angela got up slowly, closed the door, and came toward Marcus. "I'll untie you. Then I'll call the police."

"No."

"What?"

"Don't untie me, just call the police."

"I don't understand."

"Just do it."

"All right," Angela said, and complied with his strange request. Since Robert had used the cord to tie up Marcus, Angela used the phone in Robert's office. After speaking to the police and reporting the murder, Angela returned to Marcus. "What now?"

"Now you've got to trust me. You have to do exactly what I say. Can you do that?"

"Yes. You're all I have now."

"Good, 'cause we don't have time for questions. Get the keys from my pocket and take the briefcase and put it in my trunk."

"Okay."

"Quickly. And come right back."

"All right, all right." Angela got the key, and did as she was instructed, but thinking that blindly following a man's instructions was what got her in this mess in the first place. Before Angela put the metal case in Marcus's trunk, she opened it.

"Oh, shit," she said as she saw the money. Angela closed the case quickly and went back inside wondering how much money it was, and what Marcus planned to do with it.

When she came back inside, Angela said, "That's done, what now?"

"When they get here the first responders won't ask you many questions. Just tell them the truth, when Robert opened the door he was shot."

"I can do that."

"Now, I'm gonna do what I can for you to avoid talking to any detectives tonight, but if you have to, you tell them what you know about the night Floyd was murdered. Tell them that we came here to find some information and that's when you found the program on Robert's computer. Without going into too much detail, explain the significance of it. You tell them that Robert came back, and caught us."

"That's when he tied you up." Angela smiled.

"You're learning. After he tied me up, Robert told you that after you left Floyd he went back and killed him. But you don't mention anything about Floyd selling the program to terrorists, or that Robert killed one of them tonight."

"What about you? How do I explain why I left you tied up? And why am I not untying you?"

"Because my being tied up adds credibility to

your story. I'll explain that I told you not to untie me so you wouldn't disturb the crime scene. Just do what I said and you'll get through this, but you have to sell it."

"I can do it, Marcus. I can sell anybody on anything," Angela said, and flashed her power smile.

"Yeah, I heard that about you."

"What do you mean by that?"

"It's nothing really, just something Pryor told Garrett he observed about you."

"What was that?"

"He said that you were the kind of woman that could answer all his questions without giving him any information."

Angela frowned. "I'm not sure I like the sound of that."

"You couldn't, but just prove him right."

Chapter 22

The first thing Marcus did when the first responders arrived at the crime scene and untied him was call Lawrence Rietman. He was a special agent with the FBI that Marcus had met during the Ferguson investigation. Once he explained the situation, Special Agent Rietman said he'd be there as soon as he could.

"Until then, cooperate with the police, but make sure your client doesn't mention anything you just told me."

"Taken care of," Marcus said, and ended the call.

After talking to Marcus, Agent Rietman made a few calls to get up to speed. When Marcus told him that the bureau was involved in the investigation of Stephanie Covey, he knew it was due to Integrated's involvement with defense contracts. The agent assigned to the case advised him that because of his involvement with the extremely sensitive project, the murder of Chuck Prentice raised a red flag, and when Stephanie Covey was murdered they began looking at Robert, but they were unaware of Floyd Dorsey.

When the Atlanta police detectives spoke with Angela, she told them exactly what Marcus had told her to say. "I had been questioned in the murders of Stephanie Covey and Floyd Dorsey and had spoken to my lawyer. He advised that we come here to Robert's apartment to see what we could find out about what Robert was involved in."

"How did you get into the apartment?"

"I was his assistant, I had a key."

"What happened when Mr. Covey got here?"

"When Robert got here, he tied Marcus up."

"Why didn't he tie you up?"

"I guess he didn't feel threatened by me physically so there was no need to tie me up."

"When the officers arrived at the scene Mr. Douglas was still tied up. Why didn't you untie him?"

"I advised her not to, Detective. I thought it was more important to preserve the crime scene," Marcus told the detective.

"I see. What happened then?"

"I told him that I was a suspect in Floyd Dorsey's murder and he admitted to me that he had killed Floyd that night after I left Floyd's office."

"Did he say why he killed him?"

"Just that it had something to do with a business deal that they were involved in."

"What happened after that?"

"He was about to leave when he was shot."

"Did you see who shot him, Ms. Pettybone?" the detective asked.

"No, my back was turned. It all happened so fast. After it happened I went to the door, but I didn't see anybody."

It wasn't long after that when Rietman arrived at the crime scene. He moved quickly to separate Angela from the detectives.

Angela told Rietman everything she knew and what Robert told them before he was murdered. "Do you have any idea who the people he met with are or where I could find them?"

"No, sir. I didn't find out about him meeting them until tonight."

"Okay, Ms. Pettybone, I think I have all that I need for the time being. We'll talk about this in more detail in the morning." Rietman turned to Marcus. "Ten o'clock in my office good for you?"

"We'll be there," Marcus said, and he and Angela got up to leave.

"Ms. Pettybone."

"Yes."

"Could you give us a minute?"

"Sure," Angela said. "I'll wait for you by the car, Marcus."

"I won't be long."

Once Angela was gone, Rietman smiled at Marcus. "Mr. Douglas, I have to compliment you."

"Why is that?"

"You always seem to have the most beautiful women as clients," Rietman told him.

Marcus laughed. "Just lucky, I guess."

"I'll see the two of you in the morning. One more thing, though."

"What's that?"

"I'm not entirely convinced that she's not involved in this up to her eyeballs."

"I'll let you in on a little secret."

"What's that?"

"Neither am I. See you in the morning," Marcus said, and went to join Angela outside.

The following morning, Angela was questioned and debriefed by the FBI. At the conclusion of that session, Agent Rietman felt comfortable that Angela's involvement was minimal. Once that was behind her, Marcus set up a meeting in the conference room at his office, with Angela and all the interested police organizations.

Since Stephanie Covey's murder occurred in Marietta, the Marietta police sent the two detectives assigned to her case. Because Chuck Prentice's body was found in the West End area of Atlanta, and Robert was murdered in Atlanta, the city of Atlanta police were invited to attend. Gwinnett County police detectives Pryor and Wiggins were invited because of their interest in Angela's involvement in Floyd Dorsey's murder.

When all the detectives were present, Marcus told them that Angela would make a brief statement, detailing the events that she knew of in the murders they were investigating. "After which, you are free to ask any questions you wish. But I want to advise you that there are some questions that she has been advised by the FBI not to comment on, because of their investigation. The FBI has assured me that if you feel that any of your unanswered questions are crucial to your investigations, they will deal with those requests on a case-by-case basis. Are there any questions about the process before we proceed?"

Detective Pryor raised his hand. "Has Ms. Pettybone been given some type of immunity for prosecution by the FBI?"

"No, she hasn't, Detective. Ms. Pettybone is co-operating with the FBI in an investigation that encompasses all of your cases. Ms. Pettybone has committed no crime in the eyes of the FBI. Therefore no immunity was necessary."

"I see."

"Ms. Pettybone," Marcus said, and looked at Angela.

She read from a prepared statement after which the assembled detectives asked her questions for nearly two hours.

"If that's all the questions you gentlemen have, I think we'll call it a day. If you have any more questions, please feel free to contact my office and we'll be happy to set up an interview with Ms. Pettybone."

One by one the detectives filed out of the conference room. The last one to leave the room was Detective Pryor. He stopped at the door and looked at Marcus and then Angela. "I have to be honest with you, Ms. Pettybone. I'm not entirely convinced that you aren't responsible for Mr. Dorsey's murder. So I assure you that we'll be in touch. Mr. Douglas," Pryor said, and nodded his head before walking out the door.

It was after six in the evening when Marcus and Angela left the conference room and walked to her car.

"I want to thank you for everything that you've done for me. I know that I wouldn't have gotten through this without you."

"You don't have to thank me, Angela. That's what friends are for."

"True, but I still want you to know that I appreciate it and you," Angela said, and kissed him on the cheek.

The feeling of Angela's lips against his skin sent chills up and down his spine. Now that her case appeared to be closed, maybe they could take their relationship in the direction that he felt they both wanted it to go. "Why don't we have dinner tonight?"

"As much as I want to say yes, I need some time to sort through all this. My feelings for Robert—and my feelings for you."

"I understand, really, I do."

"I just need some time." Angela kissed him again, on the lips this time. "And besides, you are my lawyer and this is far from being over."

"That much is certain."

"I'm sure we'll be seeing a lot of each other and we'll see where it goes."

"Sounds good."

"There is one more thing that we have to talk about. I didn't want to bring it up while we were in the office. I know how the walls have ears sometimes," Angela said.

"The money."

"Have you counted it?"

"Yes. It's a million dollars, and it's in a safe place. Once this is really over we'll talk about what to do with it. But right now you showing up with a bunch of money is the last thing that needs to happen. I've got a friend in New York that may be of some help with getting the money to you without it bringing too much attention to you."

"What about you?"

"What about me?"

"I think you deserve some of it. You earned it."

"I just gave you some advice as your lawyer that got you out of trouble. I just did my job. But don't you worry, you'll get my bill."

"It's one bill I'll gladly pay." Angela kissed Marcus on the cheek again. "Thank you for everything you've done, and for being so understanding."

After seeing Angela to her car, Marcus returned to his office to make some notes on the case. While he rode the elevator up to his floor, Marcus thought about Angela and what might have been.

He opened the door to his office and went in, thinking that Angela would come around when she was ready. "I was starting to think you weren't going to come back in here." The voice came from his chair, which was facing the window.

As soon as Marcus heard the voice he knew who it was. When the chair spun around, there sat Panthea Daniels. She was dressed impeccably in a Chloé crystal silk minidress accented with plissé inserts, vinyl appliqués, and Bulgarian rose embroidery, with a touch of sparkling crystals on top. "But I knew that you always come back to your office before you leave. It gives you a chance to gather your thoughts, make some notes, and catalog any observations you have. You see, I know everything about you, lover."

"What are you doing here, Panthea?"

"I wanted to see you, Marcus. You know how much I've been missing you."

"You're supposed to be on a cruise."

"And I am. At our first stop, security was too busy flirting with me to check my ID. Or maybe it was me flirting with him? Either way, as far as they know, I'm still on the ship. We were at sea yesterday, but today we've docked in Saint Martin, and I have a full day planned. Do you remember how you and I planned to go to Saint Martin, before you lost your mind and threw me away like I was garbage?"

Marcus started backing up toward the door. "Where are you going, lover?" Panthea said, and pulled a gun from her handbag.

"From the looks of things, I'm not going anywhere, Panthea. So why don't you tell me what we're doing here?"

"Don't try to handle me, Marcus. You never were good at it."

Marcus put his hands out in front of him where Panthea could see them. He didn't want to make any sudden moves and give her a reason to shoot. "Is it all right if I sit down?" he asked, and motioned for a chair.

"No. I prefer that you stand. You know I always did like looking at you. Watching you move. Hearing that sexy voice of yours."

"I remember."

"Do you like this outfit?" Panthea asked, and stood up.

"You look very nice, Panthea."

"I knew you would like it. I got it just for you today at Saks. It cost almost six thousand dollars, but if you like it, it was worth every dollar. Do you still like looking at me, Marcus?" Panthea came around from behind the desk, so he could see her in the outfit.

"Yes."

"I knew you did. It just took you a while to remember, but I promise not to hold it against you."

"You still haven't told me what we're doing here."

"I don't even know if that's a question. Are you asking me, or are you just pointing out the fact that I haven't broken it down for you? But I shouldn't have to, because it's really quite obvious."

"Tell me anyway."

"I'm going to kill you, Marcus. Because like they say, if I can't have you, then I guess I have to make sure that nobody can."

"It's been you, hasn't it?"

"You mean the calls, and your house, and your car? I'm afraid so."

"How'd you get in?"

Panthea looked at Marcus like he should know the answer to his question. "I have a key and the alarm code of course. What kind of woman would I be if I couldn't get into my man's house?"

"Why, Panthea? Why'd you have to do all that?"

"When you threw me away, you took everything from me. I have nothing without you. I thought that it was only fair that I return the favor." Panthea smiled. "I knew if I took everything that you had I would get your attention."

"You've got my attention now."

"No, I don't!" Panthea screamed. "She has your attention, Marcus!"

"Who are you talking about?"

Panthea pointed the gun at Marcus and he took a step back. "Don't insult my intelligence, Marcus. You know exactly who I'm talking about. You should, you've spent the last four days with her."

"She's a client, Panthea."

"I was your client!" Panthea gripped the gun a little tighter. "So tell me, Marcus, what's so special about her?"

"You've got it all wrong, Panthea, believe me. Angela and I are old friends from college. She needed my help."

"And here comes Marcus to the rescue. It's a bird, it's a plane, no, it's Superdick. Come to save another helpless female client from the forces of evil."

"It's not like that, Panthea."

"Oh, sure, and you were so involved in her case that you were at her house until I let you know it was time to go home. How many times did you make her come while you were there?"

"Panthea, please, we don't have to do this."

"Do what? Kill you? Oh yes, I do. You have got to die today, Mr. Douglas. I cannot stand by and let you do to another woman what you did to me."

"What did I do that was so wrong?"

"You loved me! And you will never love another woman again! You are mine, Mr. Douglas. You seem to have forgotten that. I stood by and let you have your fun with those others. I understood that, I know the kind of man you are. I know you had to have somebody, but I just knew that once you had had your fill of them you would realize that you and I were meant to be together. Realize that you and I are forever."

It was just then that Marcus realized that if Panthea knew of and tolerated the other woman he had seen since they separated, she had been following him for some time. "How long have you been following me?"

"I think following you is too strong a statement. It was more like I was keeping tabs on you. But make no mistake about it, I always knew where you were, what you were doing, and who you were doing it to."

"Why, Panthea?"

"Because you're mine!" Panthea shouted, but quickly lowered her voice. "Then she came along and I felt I was losing you. And it hurt me, hurt me deep in my soul. My whole body ached. I had to do something, something to get you away from her, but you kept going back to her. She couldn't possibly love you, she couldn't possibly make love to you the way I did."

"She can't, Panthea. She can't because nothing is going on between us."

"Don't lie to me! I can see it in your eyes." Panthea took a step closer. "I can smell her cheap perfume on you. I knew if I followed her that she would lead me to you."

"You followed her?"

"Of course I did. That's how I found your little love nest. I couldn't find you, but I knew she couldn't stay away from you, I knew I never could, and she would lead me right to you."

"What love nest? What are you talking about?" Then Marcus thought about it. "You followed her last night. It was you that killed Robert Covey."

"I didn't mean to kill him. I really didn't, I just shot the first one that came out that door. I just thought it would be you. I don't even know how he got by me. Unless of course he was already there and the two of you did her." Panthea paused and thought about what she just said. *How did he get past me? I was watching the door, he couldn't have gotten past me. He must have been there the whole time,* Panthea thought. "That's what happened, didn't it, Marcus?"

"What do you mean?" Marcus asked curiously.

"The two of you had her. You never did that to me." Marcus just shook his head. Slowly the expression on Panthea's face began to soften, her grip on the gun became a little looser. "Maybe I've been wrong about her. If you loved her the way you love me, you would never let another man have her."

"Panthea, please, listen to me. I don't love her. I

never have. There hasn't been, and I know there never will be, a woman to have me the way that you do," Marcus said slowly, and took a step toward Panthea. "She means nothing to me, Panthea. It's you. It's always been you. Remember, you and I are forever."

"Oh, Marcus. You say the sweetest things to me."

"I always have, Panthea. And I'm sorry. Give me a chance to make things right."

"Do you really mean that?"

"Yes." Marcus took another step. "Now why don't you put down that gun and come here so I can love you?"

Panthea looked at the gun in her hand and waved it around. "Oh, Marcus. I could never kill you. I love you too much for that," she said, continuing to wave the gun. "Just hearing you say that she means nothing to you, I could just—"

The gun went off and Marcus fell to the floor.

"Oh my God, Marcus!" Panthea screamed, and dropped to her knees. She grabbed his jacket and shook him. "Marcus! Marcus! Marcus!" she cried, and the tears rolled down her cheeks. "I'm sorry, Marcus. I didn't mean to—"

Panthea lay on the floor next to Marcus and took his hand. "I love you," she said, and put the gun to her temple. "You and I are forever," Panthea said, and pulled the trigger.

Chapter 23

Tiffanie Powers was hard at work as usual. Everyone else in the law offices of Marcus Douglas and Associates had long since gone home for the evening. But Tiffanie had a plan; she was going to be a partner.

She often thought about, and was encouraged by, a conversation she had once had with Marcus. He was preparing for a case and needed a sounding board. Marcus had come to Tiffanie. "Me?"

"You're the best lawyer I know and there is no one better at speculating on alternate theories of a crime than you," Marcus told her that day. As the conversation continued, Marcus had asked Tiffanie to turn over a case she'd been working on to another associate, but she would still be the primary lawyer and the associate would report to her. Tiffanie pointed out, "Whether you intended it to be or not, you have given me supervisory responsibilities. Or one might assume that you have, since the only one who, prior to this, had supervisory responsibilities in the office was you."

Marcus explained to her that the firm was experiencing some growth and that he was looking for somebody who was willing to step up and assume a greater role. Tiffanie, being the type of person she was, stepped up immediately.

"Some people might think that is the definition of a partner," Tiffanie remembered telling Marcus.

"Damn you're ambitious, Tiffanie. But that's the thing I liked about you right from the start. But yes, some people might think that is the definition of a partner. But let's see how this works out before we start talking 'partner.'"

She was already running the office; all the other associates reported to her and she reported directly to Marcus. Since that conversation, the P word had come up on several occasions, and Tiffanie felt it was just a matter of time before she would be called to Marcus's office and he would congratulate her on becoming his partner. It was inevitable. *Douglas, Powers, and Associates. It has a nice ring to it,* Tiffanie often thought.

On this particular night, Tiffanie was working on a draft of a motion to dismiss the robbery charges against Nadia Whitfield, who was charged with murder and armed robbery. Since Marcus had spent most of the day with Angela Pettybone and the police, she was glad to help out.

Tiffanie had just finished writing the first draft when she thought she heard a loud noise. "What the fuck was that?" she said aloud. She got up from her desk and looked out the window. Not seeing anything out of the ordinary, she went to her door and checked the hallway. Since she didn't see anybody in the hall, and knowing that most everybody had gone for the evening, Tiffanie shrugged her shoulders and returned to her desk and her work.

After saving the draft on her computer, Tiffanie got up and started preparing to leave the office for the night. She printed the draft document and was going to drop it in Marcus's box for him to review in the morning.

Tiffanie turned off her light and began going down the hallway on her way to the elevator. She had just pressed the button when she heard another loud noise. "That came from Marcus's office," she said, and moved in the direction of the sound.

When Tiffanie got to the door of Marcus's office, she tapped lightly before going in. She opened the door to his outer office where his personal assistant, Janise, sat, and didn't see anything, except she noticed the door to Marcus's office was cracked open. "Marcus," Tiffanie called to him. If he was in there, she didn't want to interrupt anything. "Marcus," she said, and slowly pushed the door.

"Oh my God!" Tiffanie screamed at the sight of Marcus and Panthea Daniels, lying hand in hand on the floor and the pools of blood that had gathered around their heads. Then she saw the gun in Panthea's hand.

"Marcus! Marcus!" Tiffanie screamed, and rushed to the phone. Her hands were shaking and she tried her best not to look at the bodies as she dialed 9-1-1.

"Nine-one-one operator. What is the emergency?"

"I just found my boss and one of his old clients, I think she shot him and then killed herself. The gun is still in her hand," Tiffanie said, and tried not to hyperventilate.

The operator took the necessary information from Tiffanie and told her she was sending a unit. As soon as Tiffanie hung up, tears began to fall. She dialed Garrett's number. "What's up, big dawg?"

"Garrett, it's Tiffanie. Marcus has been shot."

"What?"

"I found him and Panthea Daniels. She shot him, then she shot herself."

"Are you all right?"

"No," she cried a little harder. "Marcus is dead."

"Did you call the police?"

"They're on their way."

"I'll be there in fifteen minutes."

Tiffanie hung up the phone and plopped down in Marcus's chair. She wanted to do something, felt she had to do something, but knew that there was nothing she could do. Tiffanie spun around in the chair and stared out the window. In that moment she realized how her relationship with Marcus, and as a consequence her feelings for him, had changed. When she first met Marcus, she was fresh out of law school. Naturally she was excited about the opportunity, but she hoped his interest in her was more than professional. Through the years working with

Marcus, she had grown to respect and appreciate him both as a lawyer and as a man.

It felt like the right side of his head was on fire and had been hit with a cinder block, but he could open his eyes. Marcus looked next to him and saw Panthea. Her eyes were open, as was her mouth. "Panthea," he said in a whisper, and glanced down at his hand. "It didn't have to end like this, baby," Marcus said, and tried to move but his head hurt. "Ahhh."

When Tiffanie spun around, she saw Marcus's eyes. "Marcus!" She sprang to her feet and rushed to him.

Tiffanie knelt down beside him and held his head close to her. "Thank God, you're alive. Don't try to move. Garrett and the police are on their way."

"Is she—"

Tiffanie glanced over at Panthea. "I think so."

Marcus closed his eyes.

When he opened his eyes the next time Marcus was in an ambulance, and the first person he saw was Tiffanie. "Garrett. He opened his eyes," he heard her say before he passed out again.

When Marcus regained consciousness, he was in the hospital. Tiffanie and Garrett were still with him, slumped over sleeping in hospital chairs. He felt the bandage around his head. Marcus closed his eyes and could see it all, heard the gun go off, cringed when he felt the pain in his head

He thought about Panthea. It really didn't have to

go the way it did. He loved her once, and that part of him was sad that she was gone. Then the inevitable question came: *What could I have done to keep this from happening?* The answer was simple, he could have talked to Panthea. He could have tried to understand what she'd been through to get her to that point, and understand where she was. But instead he shut down, closed himself off to her, and acted like she never existed. Like the love they shared never happened. Marcus knew that he was responsible for what Panthea did, and all it would have taken to prevent it was to listen to her and talk to her.

When Marcus noticed Garrett moving in his chair, he spoke. "How long have you been here?"

"Hey," Garrett said, and shook Tiffanie. "How you feeling?"

"My head hurts, but other than that I guess I'm all right."

"The doctor said the bullet just grazed your skull. You lost some blood, but you just need to rest," Tiffanie said, and took his hand in hers.

"How long have I been here?" Marcus asked.

Garrett looked at his watch. "About eight or nine hours."

"Panthea?"

Tiffanie dropped her head and looked away.

"The paramedics weren't able to revive her. She's dead," Garrett confirmed for him.

"It was Panthea that shot Robert Covey. She followed Angela there and shot the first one out the door."

"I'll let the police know," Garrett said.

"You don't worry about that now, Marcus. You just rest," Tiffanie said to him.

"Don't worry. I'm going to take a long vacation."

"Where you thinkin' 'bout goin', big dawg?"

Marcus was thinking about what Carmen Taylor had said about coming back to the States. "New York."